**"I'll do whatever it takes to protect you. That much is true. This case has been hell."**

The weariness in his eyes caused her heart to stutter.

"I need to know you're not going to disappear on me again."

"You have my word."

If only she could be certain. "You know I love you."

"Then, believe in me. This is different."

"How? What's different this time?"

"I know what's at stake."

"But you're hiding something now."

She steadied herself for the lie.

"You're right."

If she hadn't been sitting, his admission would've knocked her off balance.

"I can't tell you everything, but as soon as this is over, I will. You have no idea how much I need you. I need to know you have faith in me."

She answered with ⬚⬚⬚⬚ ⬚⬚⬚ a silent prayer he'd come back alive.

# *GUT INSTINCT*

---

## BARB HAN

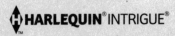
HARLEQUIN® INTRIGUE®

My deepest thanks to my editor, Allison Lyons, for challenging me
and making me a better writer. To my agent, Jill Marsal, for her
brilliant guidance and unfailing support. To Brandon, Jacob and Tori,
for encouraging me to work hard and inspiring me to dream. To my
husband, John, for walking this journey side by side with me—I love
you. And a special thank-you to readers, and especially my girlfriend's
mom, Linda Tumino, for being so very passionate about books.

ISBN-13: 978-0-373-69809-7

Gut Instinct

Copyright © 2015 by Barb Han

Recycling programs
for this product may
not exist in your area.

**Printed in U.S.A.**

**Barb Han** lives in North Texas with her husband, three beautiful children, a spunky golden retriever/poodle mix and too many books to count. When not writing, she spends much of her time on or around a basketball court. She's passionate about travel. Many of the places she visits end up in her books. She loves interacting with readers and is grateful for their support. You can reach her at barbhan.com.

## Books by Barb Han

## Harlequin Intrigue

*Rancher Rescue*

**The Campbells of Creek Bend**
*Witness Protection*
*Gut Instinct*

# CAST OF CHARACTERS

***Julie Davis (formerly Julie Campbell)***—She owns a landscaping business. When one of her appointments causes her to interrupt a serial killer, he'll set his sights on her to finish the job.

***Luke Campbell***—Most of this FBI agent's young career has been spent tracking a vicious serial killer. When the path leads him to the last place he expects, his ex-wife, he'll learn exactly how much he's willing to risk to save the woman he still loves—even if he's left devastated a second time around.

***Nick Campbell***—This US marshal is a phone call away when his brother needs help. He's willing to do whatever it takes to help track down the killer.

***Reed Campbell***—This Border Patrol agent will do anything to help his brother in his time of need. He has no qualms about using all his resources, either.

***Detective Garcia***—The detective and Luke are working together to rid North Texas of a deranged killer. But when he gets too close, his own life is put on the line.

***Chad Devel***—This twentysomething sous chef is a charmer who likes to party. But is he the killer known as Ravishing Rob, the murderer who captivates then decapitates?

***Rick Camden***—Chad's half brother fits the profile of the serial killer, but the logistics don't work. Could he manage to be in two states at once?

***Bill Hightower***—This reporter is a little too eager to score an interview with the FBI agent. Is he more involved than he's willing to admit?

# Chapter One

Luke Campbell bit back a groan. Why did Julie Campbell—correction, Julie *Davis*—have to interrupt a killer in the middle of one of his "projects"?

His ex-wife's landscaping business had brought her to the doorstep of one of the most devious serial murderers in Luke's career. A knot tightened in his gut as he pulled in front of her small redbrick town house in a North Dallas suburb, the one they'd shared, and parked his truck.

An emotion he refused to acknowledge kept him from opening the door and stepping into the frigid night. How many times had he wished he still lived in that house after he'd come home from active duty a wreck? How many times had he prayed he could go back and change the past since then? How many times had he missed the feel of her long silky legs wrapped around him, welcoming him home? *Too many.*

Hell, he wasn't there for a reunion. She was in jeopardy, and his job was to protect society from national-security threats and major criminals. Keeping her safe was the least he could do after the way he'd hurt her.

He stepped into the crisp evening air.

A young detective with a thick build and sun-worn face approached. "Evening, Special Agent Campbell. Not sure if you remember me, but I worked the Martin crime scene earlier."

"Detective Wells. Thank you. I appreciate the call." Luke shook the outstretched hand in front of him.

"I wouldn't normally bother you with something like this. My boss thought you'd be interested."

The young guy reported to Detective Garcia. Garcia's judgment was dead-on. "What do you have?"

He waved another detective over. "This is Detective Reyes."

Luke shook hands with the detective.

·"Show him what was taped to Ms. Davis's window earlier," Detective Wells said.

The officer used tongs to hold out a standard-size piece of white paper. The words *I hope you enjoy your dance with the Devil. Be in touch soon, Rob* were handwritten.

"Whoever wrote this has good penmanship." Luke noticed. He took note of the capitalization of the word *Devil*. The tension between his shoulder blades balled and tightened as he reread the name. His killer, Ravishing Rob, never left a clue as to whom he would target next. If this was him, why would he change his M.O.?

One reason came to mind. Anger. Rob was meticulous. Julie had interrupted his ritual killing, which he'd described as more of a turn-on than sex. That might be enough to trigger a variation.

Luke couldn't ignore another possibility. This could be a copycat. Julie's picture had been splashed all over the news and internet.

Then again, Julie had black hair just like all Rob's targets.

He examined the neat print. Cursive would give more clues to Rob's personality. With his high IQ he was smart enough to know that, too, which made the capitalization of *Devil* even more poignant. "Whoever wrote this took his time."

Luke pulled an evidence bag from his glove box and pointed at the note. "I'll send this up for analysis."

The detectives nodded.

"Can you spare one of your uniformed men for the night? I'd like someone to keep watch on the alley behind her house."

"Sure thing," Detective Wells said. "I made some notes after interviewing Ms. Davis. Do you want to take a look?"

"Absolutely." Luke studied the page. He focused on the word *boyfriend*. The knot tightened in his gut. The thought of another man's arms wrapped around Julie ignited his possessive instincts. He still wanted her, needed her. Those selfish emotions had caused him to stay at the town house to be near her when he'd returned from Iraq a broken man. The front-row seat he'd had to her pain—the hell he'd caused—when he pushed her away day after day had forced him to man up and leave before he permanently damaged her. Intelligent and beautiful, she deserved so much more than him. He glanced up at the detectives who were waiting for his response to the report. Not wanting to give away his bone-deep reaction to her, he skimmed the rest and handed it back. "Good information. Send my office a copy of the report when it's filed."

Detective Wells gave a satisfied smile. "I'll keep a man outside tonight. Let me know if you need anything else."

"Will do." Luke turned and walked toward the house. A thought stopped him at the base of the stairs. What if she wasn't alone?

The detective's notes said she'd been dating a dentist on and off. Was he here?

Davis had been her maiden name, which meant she was still single. Even so, she might be *on* with the dentist again. After the day she'd had, he might be there with her in Luke's house. *Old house,* he corrected, ignoring the all-too-real tug of emotion at seeing the place again.

Taking the couple of steps to her porch in quick strides, he clenched his fists.

The thought of Ravishing Rob targeting Julie didn't do good things to Luke's head. He knocked on the door and his chest squeezed as he thought about seeing her again.

The solid hunk of wood swung open, and suddenly, there she was, his ideal combination of beauty and grace, staring at him with a shocked look on her face. He could see those long legs where her bathrobe split, her taut hips where the robe cinched. A hunger roared from deep within him. The reality of why he was there chased it away.

Her amber eyes stood out against pale skin. Even red-rimmed and puffy, their russet-coppery tint was every bit as beautiful as it had been the last time he'd seen her. Her shoulder-length hair was still inky black. His fingers itched to get lost in that curly abyss again. Muscle memory, he decided. Besides, the frown on her face and stress in her eyes said he was the last person she wanted to see.

Under the circumstances, he was her best bet.

She opened her mouth to speak, but her ringtone sounded. "Dammit. Hang on."

Bad sign. She only cursed when she was hanging on by a thread.

"May I?" He motioned for permission to enter.

Her gaze narrowed, but then she nodded and turned her back to him. She spoke directly into the phone. "I'm okay. No. I promise. You don't need to come over right now. I'll see you when you get off work."

Was she talking to her boyfriend? The last word stuck. Tasted bitter as hell, too.

One step inside and he almost lost his footing. A wave

of nostalgia slammed into him. The furniture was in exactly the same spot as when he'd left. The coffee-colored leather sofa against the wall to his right. The flat-screen directly across from it mounted on the wall to his left. He could see all the way to the back door from where he stood. Same black pedestal dining table with avocado-green chairs tucked around it. The place looked completely untouched, except all the pictures of the two of them had been removed. She'd probably enjoyed stomping on the frames.

The town house might've looked the same, but it had a different air. Funny how out of place he felt in what used to be his own home.

He folded his arms, parted his feet in an athletic stance and stood next to the door. He wasn't there for a reunion. This was business. And no matter how much Julie looked as if she'd rather crawl out of her skin than be in the same room with him, he had a job to do.

She closed the call and whirled around on him, still wearing her angry expression. There was something else in her eyes there, too. Hurt? "Why did they send *you?*"

"I've been tracking this guy for the past two years. He's my case." He intentionally withheld the part about Ravishing Rob being the most ruthless killer Luke had come across so far in his FBI career.

Her eyes narrowed to such slits he couldn't figure out if she could see him anymore. Then again, she probably wanted to block him out altogether, and he couldn't blame her. She'd pleaded with him to stay, but he couldn't stand watching her pain when he had no way to heal either one of them.

With all the daggers shooting from her eyes, he couldn't tell if she was using anger to mask other emotions. Hurt? Fear? Regret?

"There's no one else they could've sent?" The hollow sound in her voice practically echoed.

"I'm afraid not."

"So the note's from him? You're sure?"

"I need to get a little more information from you to help me decide." Even though she'd already given her account to police and he'd read the jacket, he needed to hear her words. He needed to know what she thought she saw. Maybe she'd remember something that could help put this monster away or help Luke figure out if it was a copycat. "Tell me what happened when you arrived at the scene of the murder this morning."

She shivered, looked lost and alone. "My client Annie Martin wanted to meet with me to discuss landscaping after her new pool was installed. I brought a rendering with me and planned to give my presentation. It was a big project that would start in the spring, so I broke all the planting down into zones." She glanced up at him curiously as if she realized he didn't know the first thing about plants or landscaping, or care. "Sorry, I'm babbling. I'm sure you didn't come here to talk about the details of my business."

"I did," he said quickly. He covered a crime scene the same way, broke it down on a grid. "I want to hear everything even if you don't think it's important. You never know what might spark a memory. Something you didn't think of before when you talked to the police." His hopes she'd be more comfortable talking to him had diminished the second he saw her. He wanted to ask her how she was doing, but decided not to, even though he found he still really wanted to know, needed to know. He'd left things broken between them, and thoughts of the sadness in her eyes every time she'd looked at him still haunted him. Outside of this case, he had no right to know anything about her. Why was he already reminding himself of the fact?

"As soon as I pulled up to her house, I heard a noise. Like a muffled cry or something. I couldn't make it out for sure. She'd asked me to come around back in case she was with contractors for the pool, so I ran to make sure she was okay. I thought maybe she tripped or was hurt. But there was no one out there. She screamed again and I ran to the front door. Someone bolted from around the side of the house about the same time. He killed her, didn't he?"

He locked gazes with her and wished like anything he could protect her from the truth. He felt pained that she'd had to witness this and his heart went out to her. "Yes. You get a good look at him?"

"No." She hugged her arms to her body. "I didn't see anything. By then I heard an awful sound coming from inside. Sounded like an animal dying." She shivered.

He pulled out a pad and scribbled notes. Not that he needed a piece of paper to remember the details of their conversation. His memory was sharper than a switchblade. He needed something to look at besides her fearful eyes. Old instinct kicked in and he wanted to maim the person who'd made her feel that way, offer comfort she would certainly reject. "What happened next?"

"You want to sit down?" She moved to the couch and sat on the edge. She clasped her hands together and rocked back and forth. "It was bad, Luke."

The sound of his name rolling off her tongue was a bitter reminder of the comfort and connection he hadn't felt in a long time. He took a seat next to her but not too close.

Tears spilled down her cheeks. "I don't want to think about it again, let alone say the words out loud."

"I know how hard this is." Every muscle in his body tightened from wanting to reach out and comfort her. He didn't want to press further, but the information he gained could mean saving her life. "It's important you tell me everything. Do you want a cup of tea or something?" He made a move to stand.

"No. I'm fine." The uncertainty in her words made him freeze.

"Anything else you can give me might save another woman from going through this."

"We both know he's going to come after me next." Her voice shook with terror.

"I'm not certain it's him yet. Besides, I'll catch him first."

The suggestion of depending on him for anything after the way he'd hurt her set her eyes to infernos. "I didn't ask you to come."

"This is my territory. My guy. I know him better than anyone else."

"I didn't even know you were FBI." The exasperation in her voice made him clench his fists involuntarily.

"I didn't think it was appropriate to send you Christmas cards after your lawyer sent me papers." It was a low blow and he regretted saying the words as soon as they passed his lips. After all, he'd been the one to leave and force the divorce issue.

She looked straight through him. "I lost track of you after…"

This wasn't the time to talk about their past. It complicated the situation. He was professional enough to look beyond shared history and concentrate on doing his job. He focused his gaze on the opened laptop on the coffee table. There was a picture of Julie at the crime scene beneath the banner Breaking News. Damn. Another reminder that she'd been placed right there for the killer or any other lunatic to see.

The last time the local newspaper printed a story with the headline The Metroplex Murderer Strikes Again, Rob went off. He'd left a message on Luke's cell complaining about how common that made him seem. Luke still hadn't figured out how the man got his number. The man calling himself Ravishing Rob—someone who captivated and then decapitated—had done his research. Efforts to trace the call were futile. He'd used a burn phone. Rob was thorough. He also knew how to play the media.

Reporters had their uses. In this case, they might've issued Julie a death warrant. "You said earlier you didn't get a good look at him. Any idea as to general information like height? Build? Race?"

She shook her head. "I was so horrified. The whole thing shocked me. One minute I was planning to meet a client, like usual, and then I thought the worst-case scenario was that I'd walked into a robbery in progress. The next thing I know, I'm staring at a person whose throat had been slit. I'll never forget her eyes, pleading." She shivered again and tears streamed down her cheeks.

Luke had to grip the pencil tighter to stop himself from wiping them away. He didn't like seeing her cry. He'd seen those tears enough for a lifetime. If it didn't mean saving her life, he'd stop questioning. "When did you find the note?"

"This evening. I'd just gotten home from spending the day at the police station answering questions."

"What time?" he pressed. She might not have gotten a good look at Rob. Rob didn't know that. The reason he'd given himself the nickname Ravishing Rob churned in Luke's thoughts as he sat next to her. Rob had said he charmed his way into his victims' homes or cars before taking them hostage, torturing them and then beheading them with surgical precision. The bastard would never get the chance with Julie, no matter how much swagger he thought he had.

"I'm not sure. All I wanted to do when I first got home was take a shower and get out of those clothes I'd been wearing. I ate dinner alone, a bowl of soup. I decided to slip out and check the mail…and that's when I saw it."

He already knew she'd showered. The smell of her pineapple-and-coconut shampoo filled his senses when he breathed. That she'd eaten alone soothed a part of him it shouldn't. He scooted back and scribbled approximate times on his notepad. "Did you see any cars?"

She shrugged noncommittally, leaning into him for support. The vulnerability in her amber eyes ripped right through him. Damned if the past didn't come flooding back all at once, reminding him of old times they'd shared and the feelings he missed.

He had to remind himself their history wasn't the reason she was leaning on him now. She was scared.

"I'm not sure. You know how this street is. There's always someone parked out there. I didn't pay attention." She tapped her hand on her knee.

"I need you to think."

"I said I didn't know," she barked in the way she did when her nerves got the best of her.

Everything about her body language said she'd just frozen up on him. Fear could paralyze victims. Once the shock wore off, she'd forget. As it was, he had very little to go on. Anything she could give him might paint a more detailed picture, save her life. The profiler had said Rob probably kept something from each of his victims and liked to hunt. A saw was his favorite weapon, but he used guns when necessary to kill them before cutting their throats. He was also a perfectionist. Rob was most likely educated, a collector, and he had weapons. "Dammit, Julie. This is important."

"Don't you have anything from the scene you can use to figure out who it is? Hair sample? DNA?"

"Doubt it. The house is being combed, but I'm not expecting the crew to find anything. This guy's careful, meticulous. Even though you interrupted him, he had the presence of mind to ensure he didn't leave a witness." He didn't tell her the guy normally cut off the heads of his "projects," as he called them. Or about the half-open carton of orange juice they'd found sitting on the counter. Since Rob wasn't able to bleach his victim this time, maybe he'd left behind a print. Doubtful, but Luke hadn't given up hope completely. "A rookie was first on the scene. That doesn't help. I just came from there. If there was evidence, which I doubt, it's most likely gone." He stabbed his fingers through his hair. "Can you think of anything else? Anything different. Doesn't have to be about what you saw. Could be anything about the visit."

Julie's gaze widened. "I was supposed to meet with her on Thursday. She changed our appointment last minute."

"Did you mention that to the police?"

"No. I didn't think about it until just now."

Bingo. New information. "Did she say why she moved the appointment?"

"No. She sent me a text asking if I could come a day early. Said something came up last minute and she needed to leave town right away."

"How long did you have the original appointment on your calendar?" This guy watched his "projects" carefully. Hacked into their computers. Studied their movements. He knew them as intimately as he could without ever having met them face-to-face. At least in this case, he wasn't monitoring her phone.

"Weeks."

Must've been the change in schedule. Damn, if Julie

had just kept the original appointment she'd be in the clear.
This guy didn't like an audience. He was most likely planning a way to finish his interrupted work…on Julie. Then
again, any crazy with internet access could be targeting her
right now. Luke glanced around. "How safe's the neighborhood?"

"I had an alarm installed after you left…"

He'd noticed the keypad earlier. "I think it's best if you
stay with a friend for a while."

"I've already thought about that. I have someone coming over later to stay the night."

"Who?" He told himself the only reason he'd asked was
to make sure it was someone who would have her back
if the killer decided to strike. Not that Luke planned on
being far away.

"A friend."

He said a quick prayer it was a female. The thought of
another man sleeping in his bed shot a lightning bolt of
anger down his spine. "Does this *friend* have a name?"

"Alice."

Relief he had no right to own washed over him. Alice
hated him. But she was a helluva lot better than Herb, the
dentist. "What time is she coming over?"

"She works until…" Julie checked her watch. Her hand
shook. "Actually, she should be getting off soon. I'll give
her a call."

Before he could debate his actions, he covered her hand
with his. A current he refused to acknowledge pulsed up
his arm. He didn't want to offer to stay in a place that
brought back so many painful memories. He couldn't count
how many times they'd made love on this very couch before he shipped off. Or how cold the leather was against
his skin when he slept there every night after his return.

"I doubt anything will happen tonight. He'll want time to regroup. I'll be right out front as precaution."

"All night?"

"Yes. I have an officer stationed out back, too." Luke was almost certain she wanted to poke his eyes out for ever having to look at him again. She still looked damn sexy. Her robe opened just enough for him to see she wore his old AC/DC T-shirt to bed. And since every muscle in his body screamed to reach out and touch her, he figured he'd better put a brick wall between them for safety's sake.

"With this cold front it'll be twenty degrees after the sun goes down. I can't let you do that. You'll freeze to death."

"I'll keep the heat on in my truck."

"It just seems silly for you to be out there when you could set up right here."

She must be awfully scared to make that offer. "I'm pretty certain I'm the last person you want to see. Let alone have sleeping under the same roof."

She folded her arms. He could've sworn he saw a flash of regret or sadness darken her features. "True."

He made a move to stand. Her hand on his arm stopped him. An electric volt shot through him, warming places it shouldn't.

"I thought if I ever saw you again, it would be for different reasons." Her lip quivered, but she compressed her mouth. Damn, it was still sexy when she was being stubborn.

"Yeah. Me, too. For the record, I don't like this any more than you do." Scratch that. He liked this situation boatloads less than anyone possibly could, even her. He'd be lying if he didn't admit to fantasizing about meeting up with her again once he got his head screwed on straight. This scenario had never once entered his imagination.

"Luke."

"Yeah."

"You look…better. I hope you don't mind me saying so."

He smiled and meant it. For some reason those words mattered to him.

"And you seem different now," she said. A melancholy note laced her tone.

The anger was gone from her voice completely now, but the sadness was far worse. Anger he could handle, fight head-to-head. He understood anger. Her sounding broken was a sucker punch to his solar plexus.

Her world had been turned upside down. She was reaching for comfort. He was still the same man she'd wanted to gut a few minutes ago. "Everyone changes a little, right?"

"Nope. Not everyone."

Was she referring to herself or Herb?

Reminders that he had no right to care didn't hold weight. He stood and walked to the door. "I'll check in with the officer stationed out back before I take my post."

## Chapter Two

The last person Julie wanted to see after the hell she'd been through today was her ex-husband. How long had it been? Three years? Four?

Worse yet, the deep timbre in his voice still caused her nerves to fizz and her body to hum. The effect he'd had—correction, *still* had—on her was infuriating and not to mention completely out of place under the circumstances.

His expertly defined muscles on a six-foot-one-inch frame made for an imposing presence. Those golden eyes, light brown curly hair, dimpled chin and cheeks brought back memories of lying in bed long after she woke just so she could watch him sleep. Her body reacted to that.

Besides, *that* was a lifetime ago.

Her cell vibrated. She read the incoming text. Alice was on her way. *Good.*

Julie heated water in the microwave and made a cup of chamomile tea to calm herself and give her something to do besides think about her ex. Hadn't she spent enough time trying to get over him? And she was almost certain she had.

*Almost.*

She threw on a pair of yoga pants and curled up on the couch with the steaming brew. She was less than thrilled her ex had shown up. Even so, she wasn't stupid. He was FBI. She'd do whatever he said to stay alive.

There was some relief that he looked better than when he'd come back from Iraq. Then he'd been a shell of the once-charismatic, -vibrant and -sexy-as-hell man he'd been.

She still remembered the day she'd learned his tour was finished and he'd be coming home. She'd sat on this very couch, where they'd made love more times than she could count, and cried tears of joy.

Nothing had prepared her for the day Luke walked through that door.

She hugged the pillow into her stomach and took a sip of her hot tea.

The cool, courageous and fearless man she'd once stayed up all night talking to was gone. He looked as if he hadn't eaten or shaved or slept in weeks. His eyes were deep set. He'd been dehydrated, starved or both. He barely spoke when he walked through the door and then folded onto the couch.

His vacant expression had startled her the most.

He'd refused to talk. The only thing she knew for sure was something very bad had happened overseas. Her determination to be there for him solidified even though he gave her zero reasons to hang on. Julie Campbell didn't quit. Her father had sown those seeds years before and the crop was fully grown.

Even though Luke had shut her out completely, she was convinced she'd break through and find the real him again. The days had been long and fruitless. Then there were the nightmares. He'd wake drenched with sweat but refusing to talk about it. The slightest noise sent him to a bad place mentally—a prison, one he wouldn't allow her access to.

She held on to their relationship, to the past, as long as

she could before there was nothing left between them but sadness and distance. Then he left.

Seeing him now, he looked different but stronger.

She sank deeper into the couch.

Living on his own must agree with him.

She heard a noise from out back and fear skittered across her nerves. She told herself to calm down. There was a police officer stationed out there and Luke covered the front. No one could hurt her. She was safe. Luke wouldn't allow anything to happen to her.

Even so, a warning bell sounded inside her. She turned out the light in the living room, slipped next to the curtain and peeked out the window. Luke's truck sat out front. Empty. He should be at his post by now. Where was he?

A knock at the back door caused her to jump.

Adrenaline had her running toward the kitchen, needing to know if Luke was there.

The tapping on the door increased and intensified, causing her heart to lurch into her throat.

She forced her rubbery legs to carry her the rest of the way into the kitchen.

"Julie" broke through the pounding noise. Luke's voice gave her strength to power forward.

She cracked the door.

He forced it all the way open and pushed his way inside. His weapon was drawn as he leaned his shoulder against the door for support. His dark eyes touched hers. "Thank God you're safe."

"What happened, Luke? What's wrong?"

"He's here." He tucked her behind him.

A scuffle sounded from the alley. Luke opened the door and bolted toward it.

Julie fought to keep pace, pushing her legs until her lungs burned.

They stopped at the sight of an officer's body lying twisted on the concrete, his radio the only noise breaking through the chilly air.

"Stay right behind me," Luke instructed as he scanned the alley for a threat, his weapon leading the way. "And watch for any movement around us."

She looked everywhere but at the officer, who she feared was too quiet to still be alive. She said a silent prayer for him.

When Luke had checked behind garbage cans and gaps in fences, he moved to the injured man. He dropped to the ground, bent over the officer and administered CPR as Julie kept a vigilant watch.

Luke leaned back on his heels after several intervals of compressions. He looked at her again and his horrified expression almost took her breath away.

"What else can we do? We can't leave him."

"There's nothing we can do now. I tried to revive him. He's gone." The sadness in his voice was palpable as he called it in. He glanced at the officer's empty holster and looked around. "His gun is missing."

A sob broke through before Julie could suppress it.

"We have to go," he said, then twined their fingers.

She noticed blood on his shirt and arms. She stuck close behind him as they bolted back through her house and toward the front door, his gun drawn.

"Alice is on her way," she said.

"We'll call her from my truck and tell her to turn around. I already notified local police. We can't stay here."

By the time they got to the front door, the silhouette of a man appeared against the front window.

Luke's grip tightened on her fingers, and he leveled his weapon at the man's chest.

Julie didn't realize she was holding her breath until the

squawk of a police radio on the other side of the door broke the silence.

Luke tucked her behind him, placing his body between her and the officer, and opened the door. He pointed to the badge clipped on his belt. "I'm Special Agent Campbell, and I called for backup. Where'd you come from? I didn't hear your sirens."

"I received a call of an officer down and was told to proceed with caution until others arrived at the scene. I was nearby."

"He's in the alley," Luke said.

The officer thanked Luke, hopped off the porch and disappeared.

Several squad cars roared up the narrow street, descending on the once-quiet neighborhood in a swarm.

Relief washed over Julie. She glanced up in time to see Alice running toward them, looking panicked.

Julie let go of Luke's hand and embraced her friend on the stairs.

"What in hell is going on?" Alice demanded.

"He was here." Another sob broke through.

Alice's expression dropped in terror. "You don't mean…? How does he know where you live?"

"I don't know. He left a note on my window earlier and now a police officer is dead."

"What note?"

"I was planning to tell you about it when you got here. We weren't sure it was him before." Julie caught her friend giving Luke the once-over.

"That who I think he is?" Disdain parted her lips as her gaze stayed trained on Luke.

Julie nodded.

"What's he doing here?"

"This is his case. He's been tracking this guy for the

past two years. He's the expert, so he's in charge." Julie hoped her friend didn't pick up on the change in her voice every time she spoke about her ex.

"Well, he isn't doing a very good job." Alice spoke loud enough for him to hear.

Julie took her friend arm in arm and turned to face the street, walking down the couple of steps to the sidewalk. "You can't know how much I appreciate you for coming. I didn't realize how dangerous this was when I called you earlier. I wasn't thinking straight. You have to go."

"Wait a minute. Are you worried about that killer coming after me, too?"

"I don't know what could happen next. This whole experience is surreal and I don't want to take any chances." Julie wished she could wake up from this nightmare. Except a little piece of her felt a sense of peace at seeing Luke again. She told herself it was only because she had to know he was all right. After the way they'd left things, she couldn't let him go completely.

"I'd feel better if you stayed with me for a few days," Alice said.

"It's safer for both of us if I stay with Luke. I'm sure he'll find this guy, and when he does, I can have my life back."

"How can you stand to be around him after what he put you through?" Alice asked, incredulous.

"It's different. This is work and our past is behind us," Julie lied. One glance in his direction released a thousand butterflies in her stomach. She rationalized the only reason that still happened was because her body remembered the passion between them. Their sex had surpassed earth-shattering, world-exploding-into-a-thousand-flecks-of-light hotness. The physical had never been an issue. She'd even lured him into bed one more time before he left, hoping they could build from there. The sex blazed, but after was all wrong.

They never got closure on their emotional connection, she reasoned. At least she hadn't. He, on the other hand, looked to be doing just fine.

Maybe a part of him regretted the quick marriage?

Whatever had happened overseas could've expedited his realization they were two strangers who had jumped too quickly into a lifetime commitment. Young people were known to be impetuous with their decisions, hearts.

Alice stared intently at Julie for a few seconds that seemed to drag into minutes. Then came "Well, if you're sure."

"I am."

"Don't worry about me. I'm a big girl," Alice reassured her.

"Yeah? Well, this guy won't care what you are," Julie said. The truth cut like a serrated knife. She looked to Luke for comfort, reassurance. For now, she wouldn't stress about the fact that one glance at him stopped the invisible band from tightening around her chest. Or that his touch warmed her in places it shouldn't.

"Tell me you're not staying here tonight," Alice said.

"I'm not."

Luke motioned for her to come back toward him. He hadn't stopped watching her since she'd stepped away, looking uncomfortable the second she left.

"Promise to stay safe," she said to Alice.

The short blonde nodded and gave Julie another hug.

"This will all be over soon and we'll have lunch at Mi Cocina again. Like normal people," she said. She pulled back and saw big tears filling her friend's eyes.

"Are you kidding?" Alice asked. "After this ordeal,

we're going out for margaritas. Or maybe I'll skip the mixer and go straight to tequila shots."

Julie glanced up at Luke. He'd finished his conversation with the officers but kept his distance. He looked impatient for her to wrap things up.

"Take care of yourself. I'll be in touch," she said to Alice.

Her friend started down the sidewalk.

Luke was by Julie's side in a heartbeat. He must've noticed her shivering, not from cold but from the shock wearing off, because he put his arm around her shoulders. She fit perfectly, just exactly as she remembered. Body to body, the air thinned and then thrummed. Julie ignored the familiar rush of warmth traveling over her skin and making her legs rubbery.

"Where's your friend parked?" he asked.

Julie scanned the vehicles lining the street. "I don't see her car."

"Call her back."

Last thing Julie wanted was to witness a confrontation. "Why?"

"He's around here somewhere." He skimmed the street. "Alice!"

Her friend stopped and turned.

Luke had already flagged an officer. "Do me a favor?"

"Sure thing," the cop said.

"See to it the blonde gets into her car, locks the doors, and then wait until she pulls away." He motioned toward Alice.

The officer nodded. "Sure thing."

Luke turned to Julie and said, "You okay with staying over at my place tonight until we find a suitable safe house?"

The thought of being alone with Luke at his place for

an entire night sent a very different kind of shiver down her body. She downplayed it as her being cold. Looking him straight in the eyes, she asked, "Do you really think that's best?"

He didn't answer her. He had already started walking her toward the house. "Want to grab an overnight bag?"

She nodded. He escorted her inside, washed the blood off his hands and waited while she threw together a few items to get her through the next couple of days.

"Rob's one step ahead of me, if it's him. I don't want to let you out of my sight until I'm certain you're protected," he said low, in practically a whisper, as he walked her toward his truck.

His reasoning made sense. After the way he'd been looking at her all night, she suspected he also probably felt some sense of guilt about how he'd left things before. Maybe he could catch a killer and ease his conscience at the same time.

Maybe she'd get the closure she so desperately needed.

Too many nights Luke Campbell had shown up in her dreams, charming her. If she spent the night with him, fixed the past, then maybe she'd be able to walk away clean, too. And possibly be ready to start a life with Herb. Or someone new. She doubted Herb would want to see her again after she'd told him she needed time to think.

Luke helped her into the truck and scanned the street again before he climbed into the driver's seat.

She glanced back at her once-quiet neighborhood.

People were on their porches or standing at their front windows watching the circus of lights. Police were urging them to go back inside and lock their doors. Knowing a cold-blooded killer stalked her, and seemed intent on never letting up, made blood run cold in her veins.

"Wanna scoot a little closer? You're shivering again."

"I'm fine. It's just been a long day."

He turned the heater up. "Shock's wearing off. I'm sorry this happened. If we saw each other again, I'd hoped it would be under different circumstances."

*If.* He'd clearly had no plans to seek her out. Why did that make her heart sink?

Because Luke was her only failure in life.

"Breathe in and out slowly," Luke said.

She did a few times. It helped calm her fried nerves. "Where'd you learn to do that?"

He shrugged, kept his gaze focused out the front window. "I took the military up on its offer to see a shrink. She was big on breathing."

Luke Campbell went to counseling? If he hadn't told her himself, she never would've believed it. "I'm shocked. You seemed so adamant about not involving doctors or having someone poke around in your head."

"I made a lot of mistakes when I came home from duty." A beat passed. "Some I could fix."

The power of that last sentence hit her like a tsunami. Perhaps he'd worked on the things he thought worth saving. Their marriage clearly didn't fall into that category. Anger burned through her. "When did you start therapy?"

"Not long before you... Doesn't matter. Point being, it helped." His tone was sharp, his words cutting.

"Before I what?" She couldn't let it go.

"Never mind." He flipped on the turn signal and then turned on the radio.

It was just like Luke to get all quiet as soon as they started talking about something personal. Hadn't that been the true failure in their marriage? He didn't trust her enough to open up.

Julie glanced in the side mirror. A white sedan turned

a little too quickly at the same time they did. "Has that car been following us?"

Luke's gaze narrowed as he checked the rearview mirror. "I've been keeping an eye on him."

"Good. I thought my paranoia was in high gear after the day I've had."

"Most people wouldn't be able to hold it together as well as you have today. I'm really proud of you." His voice was low and masculine, and it sent unwelcome sensual shivers racing through her.

She rubbed her arms to stave off the goose bumps.

"Hold on tight." He cut a hard right without signaling. The white sedan didn't follow.

"Looks like I was imagining things. Sorry," Julie said, ignoring the electric current pulsing through her at being this near Luke again. Damn body.

"No need to apologize. He landed on my radar, too. Besides, I want you to suspect everyone and everything around you from here on out. I want you to take every precaution until I can put this whole ordeal behind you and restore your previous life."

*What life?* She almost said it out loud. She hadn't had much of an existence since he'd walked away.

Luke glanced at the rearview mirror again.

"The white sedan just pulled up behind us."

## Chapter Three

Luke maneuvered in and out of traffic as he directed Julie to take his cell and call Detective Garcia. If this was Rob, he'd escalated to killing cops to get what he wanted, so murdering FBI wouldn't bother him.

The clue Rob had left earlier with the capitalized word resurfaced in Luke's thoughts. Nouns were capitalized. A noun could be a street name or a town. Luke thought about the word again—*Devil*. Proper nouns were capitalized, too. Could it be his last name?

Bluetooth picked up the call, and Garcia's voice boomed through the speakers. "What can I do for you?"

"I've picked up a tail. If he's not one of yours, I'm going to shake him."

"You should have a white unmarked sedan behind you to make sure you weren't being followed."

Luke glanced at the rearview mirror and caught the quick flash of headlights. "Appreciate the extra eyes. Let me know if he sees anything, will you?"

"Absolutely. I'll text any information we get. So far, he says everything looks cool. We've been interviewing Ms. Davis's neighbors. No one saw anyone suspicious around her house. Didn't hear anything, either. We'll keep on it. Any information coming in from your guys at the Martin house?"

"No word from the team. The tech guys are working on her computer. Maybe they'll get lucky and we'll get an IP address."

"That would be like Christmas morning."

"Or like seeing the Tooth Fairy," Luke agreed. "You already know about the orange juice, right?"

"He take a drink by any chance?"

"Didn't get that lucky. The container was left out half-open."

"Looks like we might have a diabetic on our hands."

"My thoughts exactly. I sent you a snapshot of the note he left behind at Ms. Davis's place. You get a chance to check it out?"

"He sure seemed to like the word *Devil,* if his capitalizing it is anything to go by. Any possibility it's an honest mistake?"

"He's deliberate. He also thinks he's too smart for us. He's been right so far. I'm hoping his arrogance will be his downfall. Any nearby towns by the name of Devil?"

"Good question. I'll have my officers check. What about a last name? We could play around with the spelling and see what comes up."

"I thought about that, too. We'll have to investigate any and all Devils in the state, plus variations. See if there are any men in their early thirties in the family. Wouldn't hurt to check for street names in Dallas, too."

"Consider it done," Garcia said. "I'll keep you posted."

Luke said goodbye and ended the call. He and Garcia had mentally connected the first time they met. They thought alike and had mutual respect for one another. The detective was a good ally to have.

Luke glanced at Julie. She gripped her elbows. "We'll get a detailed report from the evidence response team soon.

The suspect didn't get to follow his usual routine this time, so maybe he left something behind we can tag him with."

"Let's hope."

Luke needed more than optimism to find Rob.

A miracle would work.

Or just a good old-fashioned mistake on Rob's part.

Luke drove into the garage of his town house and parked. "My place isn't big. There's a decent kitchen, and coffee's always stocked."

She half smiled the way she did when she was nervous.

"Right. I forgot you don't drink coffee. Sorry, I don't have any tea."

"I drink coffee now. I only drink tea at night to help me sleep."

He cocked an eyebrow at her, remembering when he'd tried to get her to taste his and she had to hold her nose to get close. "Since when did you start drinking coffee?"

She shrugged. "I missed the smell."

He didn't know what the hell to do with that, so he took off his bloodstained pullover, discarded it and took her on a tour. He walked her through the downstairs, which had a similar layout as her place—shotgun style. "My sisters helped pick out the furniture. It's pretty basic."

"It's nice."

Why did those two words lift the heavy weight bearing down on his shoulders since the day he'd walked out? He decided to ignore it and move on.

"By the way, I thought FBI agents wore dark suits and starched white shirts."

He glanced down at his camo pants and black V-neck T-shirt. "Only the ones on TV. This is pretty standard-issue when we're combing through a crime scene."

"That where you were when they called you?"

He nodded. "I would've been by your place to talk to you tonight anyway."

Upstairs, he brought her to the guest room and stepped aside to let her lead the way. "This is where you'll sleep. I'm right next door if you need anything."

She swallowed hard, and he tried not to notice.

"I'm sure I'll be fine."

The fact that only a thin wall would separate them forced its way into his thoughts. "There's not much more than a bed in here, as you can see, but my family says it's comfortable."

"How are Meg and Lucy?"

"Fine. Meg just had a baby." It pleased him that she remembered his sisters.

Surprise widened Julie's amber eyes. "She's married?"

Being with Julie made the past few years fade away. He realized a lot had happened since they'd last spoken. "She's all grown up now with a family of her own."

"Did she have a boy or girl?"

"A boy."

"Another fine Campbell man," she noted. The pride in her tone caused Luke's chest to swell.

"He's an Evans, but, yeah, he'll always have Campbell blood running through him." He absently rubbed the scruff on his face. "He already acts like one of us. He's taken over their lives."

"Then she married Riley." A melancholy look overtook her otherwise-exhausted expression. "I wish I could've been there. Your sisters were always kind to me. I can't even imagine your gran's reaction to the news. She must be so proud."

"She's beside herself, all right. You know how she is. We had a big barbecue to celebrate the day he came into the world." He smiled, and a little bit of the tension from the day subsided.

"Mind if I ask his name?" She sat on the edge of the bed, folded her hands in her lap and beamed up at him.

"Henry, but we call him Hitch for the way he hitched a ride in all of our hearts." For a second, time warped. There she sat on his guest bed, wearing the AC/DC T-shirt she'd stolen from him. She'd claimed he'd broken it in for her. Conversation was easy, just like old times. He leaned against the doorjamb. Luke forgot how much he missed talking to his wife. *Ex-wife,* a little voice inside his head corrected.

As much as he wanted to stay on memory lane a little longer, he couldn't afford to get sidetracked for so many more reasons than just this case. "I should check in and see what the team has come up with. I'll be downstairs if you need anything."

Her chest deflated. "Okay."

The image of Julie on his bed in his nightshirt stirred an inappropriate sexual reaction. Luke changed his plan and headed to the shower.

The blasting cool water went straight to his throbbing midsection. He folded his arms above his head and braced himself against the wall, allowing water to cascade down his back. He closed his eyes and concentrated on the case.

A distraction right now was about the worst thing. He needed to keep a clear head and his thoughts off those long silky legs of hers. Of course, his body screamed accomplishing that feat would be easier said than done with her under the same roof.

A serial killer wanted to stop her heart from beating, he reminded himself.

He let the thought sit for a minute, bearing the full weight of the returning rock.

The shower helped him refocus. Luke toweled off and threw on boxer shorts and a T-shirt.

Downstairs, he made a sandwich and then booted up his laptop. Skimming through two hundred–plus emails, he took a bite and chewed.

The first email he opened was from the leader of the evidence response team. Preliminary data didn't give them much to work with, other than the orange juice. They'd combed the place in a grid, as per standard operating procedure. Nothing stood out. Didn't seem to help that he hadn't had time to spread bleach everywhere, and especially on the victim. They'd pulled carpet fibers anyway. They'd taken photographs and diagrammed the scene. If they found anything useful, Luke would be the first to know, the team leader promised.

Luke scanned emails for Garcia's name or anything from tech.

Nothing yet on either count.

His cell phone buzzed. He moved to the table and retrieved it.

There were eight texts. They must've come in while he was in the shower. He scrolled through them and stopped at Garcia.

His message said there were no cities or residents named Devil in the state of Texas. But there were twenty-four people in Texas with the last name Devel.

Luke texted Garcia. Excellent. We can split the list and start from there.

Garcia pinged back immediately. I'll email the names and addresses.

Luke replied. I'll take the bottom half.

He thumbed through the rest of his messages. Most were from his family. There was a new picture of Hitch. A pain hit hard and fast looking at the little boy's round cheeks and toothless smile. For a split second, Luke wondered if his and Julie's baby would look like his nephew.

Shaking off the thought, the ache in his chest, he moved to his laptop.

In the system, he pulled up the email from Garcia and scanned all twelve names. He printed the list. Three were female. He'd pay them a visit anyway in case one had a brother, husband or father sharing the name. He put a question mark by their names.

One Devel was dead. He crossed out that entry. Eight names drew more interesting possibilities. Two weren't far. They lived in Addison and Dallas. The other names came from Austin, San Antonio and Houston. He could drive a circle. It would take only a couple of days max to investigate everyone on his list.

They'd start tomorrow.

Since both of his brothers worked in law enforcement, a U.S. marshal and a Border Patrol agent, Luke sent the list to them, as well, asking for background checks, paying special attention to anyone in the medical field.

The stairs creaked and Julie stepped into the room. "Just wanted a glass of water. Hope that's okay."

"Help yourself." He motioned toward the kitchen. Being around her, especially at night, made him want things he shouldn't. He kept his gaze focused on the monitor, where it belonged.

She poured her drink. "Not sure if I can sleep just yet. Mind if I sit?"

"Not at all," he said, but his brain protested. If she knew how his body went on autopilot sex alert every time she was near, he wondered if she'd run. He also wondered if she still made that sexy little groan when he traced his finger behind the back of her knee.

She took a seat across the dining room table from him. "Find anything interesting?"

He glanced up and his heart squeezed. "Not yet. Garcia sent a list of names. We're going on a road trip tomorrow to investigate a list of people who have a last name spelled *D-e-v-e-l*."

"How'd you get that name?"

"From his note. He capitalized the name Devil. We ran variations and this is the best match."

"Sounds promising."

"Might not be anything." They were playing probabilities. The real reason the letter *d* had been written in uppercase could mean something else entirely. Yeah, a copycat. Or Rob could simply be playing with them, waving that big IQ like a you're-an-idiot flag.

She took a sip of water.

He didn't want to get her hopes up, considering they had little to go on. "We don't know if it'll lead anywhere just yet." He looked into her amber eyes and saw that the color had deepened, the way it did when he brushed his lips across hers. Damn.

What time was it?

He glanced at the clock, needing a reality check.

"It's well after midnight," she said, her voice almost a whisper.

"We need to get on the road early tomorrow. I was hoping we could leave by six."

She gasped. "In the morning?"

He chuckled. She'd never been an early bird. Then again, he wasn't, either, when he'd had the chance to lie in bed with her, hold her, kiss her. He could lose an entire day with her in his arms. Nothing else mattered but the two of them, being together. Hell, they'd missed more than a few meals in favor of staying in bed. The war broke him of needing sleep. Broke him of a lot of other things, too.

Or maybe just broke him.

She drained her glass. "Guess I'll head upstairs."

"You want to take something to read?" he asked, remembering how she'd said it helped after he'd been deployed.

The reference didn't go unnoticed by her, as evidenced by her half smile. "I'll be okay. Thanks, though. I didn't think you remembered any of that stuff."

How could he forget? She was all he had thought about when he was locked into that hole in enemy camp.

His gaze touched hers and electricity fired through him when their eyes met. His growing erection tightened at what else he recalled about her body. "It's no big deal."

Her smiled faded too quickly as she disappeared up the stairs. "Okay."

He silently cursed himself for hurting her.

No. It was important to put some emotional distance between them. He was sliding down that slippery slope of needing her more than air again. And he'd only disappoint her.

This time, he'd be selfless. He wouldn't drag her into his crazy world only to destroy her. No matter what it cost him personally.

An hour slipped by before he looked at the clock again. He'd mapped their route and caught up on a few emails.

Checking on Julie was for work, he told himself as he walked upstairs and stood outside her door.

A muffled scream pumped a shot of adrenaline through him.

He burst into the room. "Julie?"

## Chapter Four

Luke shot through the door. "I'm here."

Julie sat bolt upright. Fear seized her lungs as the image of her client's slit throat stamped her thoughts.

Her heart raced, tears streamed, and she immediately did what she knew better than to—reached for Luke.

He was already there at her side, kneeling by the bed.

She folded into his arms, sobbing.

"You're safe. I got you," he soothed. He whispered more comforting words that wrapped around her like a warm blanket.

She pulled back. "I'm sorry. I had a bad dream. I'm fine now."

"You're drenched. Hold on." He hopped up and disappeared around the corner.

Water ran in the hall bathroom.

Returning with a cool wet hand towel, he pressed it to her forehead as he sat on the edge of the bed. "This should help."

A shiver raced through her when his finger grazed her cheek. Her pulse sped up another notch.

"Better?"

She nodded. When did he get so good at comforting others?

Whenever it was, she was grateful he was there. Dealing

with this by herself was unthinkable. Then she reminded herself that Luke was the one who'd walked out.

And yet, her body remembered his touch—the way his finger grazed the back of her knee, sending a sexual current rippling through her. Naturally her body would remember, react to him being this close. Didn't mean she wanted to peel her clothes off and let those strong arms wrap around her naked body.

Did it?

"I'll be okay." She took the hand towel from him and used it to cool the back of her neck. "What time is it?"

He retrieved his cell from the next room. "Two-thirty."

There were dark circles under his eyes. He rubbed the stubble on his chin.

"You haven't slept, have you?"

He shook his head and then stabbed his fingers through his curly hair. "Guess time got away from me. I mapped out our route for in the morning."

Even with his bloodshot eyes and stray locks, he was a beautiful man. He'd laugh at her if she said it out loud, but he was beautiful. "Can you survive on less than four hours of sleep?"

He bit back a yawn and smiled, revealing a peek at his dimples. "Yeah."

What would happen if she tried to rest again? The thought of closing her eyes didn't do good things to her imagination. The nightmare had felt so real. And yet, depending on Luke wasn't a good idea, either.

"You don't have to babysit me. I'll be okay," she said, more so trying to convince herself.

"You had a nightmare."

"I saw her…right before she… That image…her eyes… will haunt me the rest of my life."

"Wish I had some magic formula to make it all go away."

"Me, too."

"The old saying is true. Time helps. Gives perspective. Dulls the pain."

"So does a good shot of whiskey." She tried to make a joke. Lighten the mood. As it was, she would jump out of her skin if a bunny hopped out of the corner.

"Tried that, too. Doesn't work. Only makes it worse. Then you lose everything important to you." His voice was husky, low.

Was he talking about her?

"I don't run away from things that go bump in the night, Luke. I know how to stick around."

"That what you think I did? Run?"

She needed to get him out of the room because the pain in his words was a presence between them. He sounded vulnerable and she wanted to comfort him. *Her*. Comfort *him*. What a joke. He was the one who'd disappeared on her. He'd ended their marriage.

"Doesn't matter. It's history. I'll try to get some rest. If not, I'll read or something. Not like you being next to me will make much of a difference. I already know you'll leave when I need you most." She was trying to frustrate him into leaving her alone. Because, honestly, if he offered to curl up with her right then, she'd jump at the chance, which wasn't her brightest idea.

Instead of fighting back, he bent forward, clasped his hands together and rested his elbows on his knees. "I deserved that."

A knife through her heart couldn't have hurt any less than seeing the haunted look on his face. He'd been through hell in Iraq. Came home a wreck. But inside, he was always a good man.

She bit back a curse. "Luke, I'm sorry. I shouldn't have said that."

"It's okay." He didn't look at her. His gaze intensified on a patch of carpet at his feet. "I can't change the past, but I'm here now. I want to help. I don't mind keeping you company. You've been through the wringer today."

"I must look washed-out, too." The thought of him sticking around sounded a hundred warning bells inside her. And yet, it was Luke. *Her* Luke. The man who'd once made her chuck all her rules and live in the moment. Truth be known, it was the only time she'd truly felt alive.

"Not at all. You're beautiful."

Hearing him say those words made her body hum and her thighs warm. Did he see the sexual desire flushing her cheeks? "Can I keep the light on?"

"Of course you can." He repositioned himself on the bed next to her, stretched out his more than six-foot frame and linked his fingers behind his head. "Remember when scary movies used to keep you up half the night?"

"True. I always made you change the channel." She laughed, relieved at the break from her internal struggle.

"Because you didn't want the bad stuff to be the last thing on your mind before you went to sleep."

He remembered? Her heart squeezed. She had to remind herself not to get too enthusiastic. He might recall a few details from their past, but they wouldn't be together right now if a serial killer hadn't set his sights on her.

The bottom line? Luke had left and hadn't looked back.

"We could go downstairs and turn on the TV for a while." He took her hand in his. His was big and strong.

Thoughts of the two of them, up late, entwined on the couch eating pizza, popcorn and anything else that was in the kitchen after spending half the night making love assaulted her. Not a good time for that memory. Especially not with him this close—so close all she had to do was move a little bit to the right in order to touch him. "You need some sleep."

He repositioned on his side, facing her. "What I need can't be found with my eyes closed. They've been shut too long already."

Logical thought screamed for her to bolt, to get a grip on her out-of-control emotions—damn dangerous emotions that were on a runaway train aimed for a head-on collision. Because, for a second, it felt as though nothing had changed between them.

Time machines didn't exist.

There was only here and now.

"I wish it were that easy, Luke."

His hand came up to her chin and lifted her face until her eyes met his. "I'm not asking forgiveness. I'd be an idiot not to realize I'm too late. I would like a shot at friendship. Is there any chance you'd consider it?"

Her heart raced when he was this close, flooding her with doubts.

They'd jumped into a relationship with both feet first last time around. Hot, sexy feet. But feet first had turned into a nosedive toward unimaginable pain. She needed his protection and professional skill, so there was no way to get out of spending time with him. Could they take it slow and get to know each other? Her heart said no.

"I can try."

His smile shouldn't warm her and make her feel safe.

"Thank you." His low baritone goose bumped her arms. He leaned over and pressed a kiss to her forehead, not immediately pulling back.

Her pulse kicked up, and heat filled the small space between them. She could see his heartbeat at the base of his throat. The rapid rhythm matched hers.

"I want to stick around to help. Will you let me?"

She nodded ever so slightly.

He eased back to his position on his side, still facing her. "You should try to get some sleep."

"You, too," Julie said, her brilliant amber eyes wide. He missed everything about her—her musical laugh, the way her forehead wrinkled and lips pursed when she really concentrated, her compassion.

He'd been an idiot to let her go.

If he could go back and change the past, he would.

"Nah. I'll be all right." Her fear had ripped through him. "I'll stay here with you. If you don't mind."

"I would like that, actually."

He settled on top of the covers beside her as she curled up next to him.

If he were being honest, she was the one he thought about at night. She was the reason he still couldn't sleep over at a girlfriend's house. She was the reason he kept his heart behind a wall. And he had no one to blame but himself.

He'd made the offer of friendship, praying like hell he could handle it.

Julie had been nothing but sweet to him when he'd returned from the war a wreck. And how did he repay her? He'd pushed her away and ruined the best thing that had ever happened to him.

Minutes ticked by after she closed her eyes.

Her breathing slowed. Rhythmic, steady breathing said she'd drifted into sleep.

Being next to her again made his heart ache in the worst possible way. He'd been off balance ever since he'd ended their relationship. He'd convinced himself she'd be better off without him. All he'd done was hurt her. It was the only call he could make at the time. He'd been broken. Sooner or later, she would've seen it, too, and then what? She'd do the same thing his father had done when life got tough— abandon him so fast that four years later his head would still be spinning. There were about a half-dozen people Luke could trust. And most of them shared his last name. Plus, what if he hadn't come back from his mental prison? He would have been dooming her to a miserable life, too.

The decision had seemed like the kindest one he could make under the circumstances. Except that he hadn't considered what it would do to him.

Walking away from her had nearly torn him apart.

Even today, he was only half a man.

Watching her sleep brought back a flood of memories. The few years that had passed since then shriveled. Having her in his home made them disappear. He wasn't sure what was worse. That he'd been a jackass then or that he had her here but couldn't touch her. His fingers flexed and released. She had been better off without him.

He'd barely pulled himself out of the dark hole he'd fallen in when all but one of his brothers in arms had been ambushed, lined up and shot in front of him. Luke had lived. He'd wasted enough of his life cursing over that little twist of fate. Time to move on.

And now Julie was back in his life.

How many times in the past four years had he wanted to drive by their old place again? Hundreds? Thousands?

Hell, he avoided that entire section of Dallas unless he had no choice. Last thing he wanted was to bump into her at a gas station or store. Even though he always looked for her. Every time he had to be in their old neighborhood, he searched the faces of strangers. Hoped.

Figured living with the torment of never seeing her was his punishment for walking away. He'd never be good enough for her. Nor would he be able to give her what she deserved no matter how much his heart wanted to believe differently.

She made a little mewling sound in her sleep and burrowed into his side. Muscle memory had him hauling her against him, bringing her closer. She rolled onto her side and tangled her leg in his.

With her body pressed to him, rational thinking flew south. He didn't want to risk waking her by moving her, so he didn't. But with her leg wrapped around his and her full breasts against his body, he couldn't stop himself from growing hard. A few pieces of cloth kept them from touching skin to skin. Being this close to the woman he never stopped loving was worse than hell.

This new punishment was probably deserved, too. He let that thought carry him to sleep.

Luke woke, but didn't move. Julie was still asleep and he couldn't bring himself to rouse her. A deep-seated need to protect her drummed through him. Anger at Rob tore through Luke. His body went on full alert and his hands shook, similar to when he'd faced a stressful situation after the war.

"Luke, what's wrong?" Julie eased into a sitting position. The look on her face was a hard slap to reality.

"I'm okay."

"You most certainly are not." She folded her arms.

The old signs of PTSD hadn't reared their heads in two years. What was going on? Wasn't he over those?

This case, being close to Julie, had to be stirring up old feelings—feelings he didn't talk about with anyone. Even in therapy, he'd glossed over his pain. How did he begin to explain to Julie what had happened without reliving the whole experience in Iraq?

"Luke?" Her voice was unsteady. Worry lines bracketed her mouth. Her eyes pleaded with him to say something.

He eased to a sitting position and leaned back against the headrest, closing his eyes against the bright sun streaming through the window. There had been no need to close the blinds. He rarely had company. "What time is it?"

"Ten o'clock." Her voice was tentative, but she scooted next to him.

They were four hours past schedule. "My body started freaking out."

"Like before?" She wrapped her arms around him and put her head on his chest. "Your heart's beating so fast."

"Yeah." The urge to move lost to his need to hold Julie. His body still shook, but with her near, he could deal with it. With her snuggled against him, his world seemed right in ways he knew better than to trust.

She looked up at him with such compassion he almost decided talking was a bad idea. Except that he found he wanted to open up a little more.

"They got much worse. That's why I slept downstairs. I didn't want you to see my weakness."

"I hate what they did to you, Luke." She held tighter to him.

He encircled her in his arms, chastising himself for his momentary weakness. "What they did to my buddies was worse. At least I survived."

"Did you?" she asked quietly, the power of her words a physical presence in the room.

He guessed not. "I'm alive."

"Not the same thing as really living, is it?" Compassion was still in her eyes, but there was something else there, too. Desire?

Did she still want him?

"True. Which I haven't been doing a lot of without you." An impulse to lean forward and kiss her slammed into him.

Her mouth was inches from his. *Way to wreck a friendship before it got started, Campbell.*

He'd wait.

If and when the right time presented itself, he'd test to see if she still moaned when he captured her earlobe between his teeth. Or if she still shuddered when he ran his lips across the nape of her neck. The thought of all the other places he'd kissed didn't help his painful erection, which couldn't be more inappropriate under the circumstances. With Rob, Luke couldn't afford to let his guard down for a second.

"I'm so sorry, Luke. I wish I'd known." She shifted her position and ran her flat palm up his back.

"Sweetheart, I wouldn't do that if you plan to get out of bed this morning."

"Oh." Her eyes widened, and she smiled a sexy, sleepy smile. "That wouldn't do either one of us any good."

"I don't know. I think I'd rather enjoy it." He smiled.

A pink flush contrasted with her porcelain skin. "Me, too," she admitted. "Which is definitely why we shouldn't."

Probably true. Being with Julie in bed was never the difficult part. His erection throbbed harder. "Can't blame a guy for missing you."

"You missed me?" The surprise in her voice twisted his gut.

"Of course I did," he said into her mass of inky hair before kissing her forehead. "Why wouldn't I?"

"It seemed so easy for you to walk away. Never look back. I just figured you were done."

That was what she thought?

How did he explain that he'd left because he couldn't watch the hurt and disappointment play out in her eyes? That he'd known in his heart he would only make things worse for her?

"It was my fault."

"You said that before." She rolled over and tossed the covers off. "We'd better get going."

What did he say wrong? Everything *was* his fault. She didn't do anything to deserve the way he'd treated her.

How did he explain that he was trying to protect her by leaving? Maybe she didn't understand his reasoning, on some level he could see that now, but he was thinking of her at the time. He'd made the best decision he could.

"I thought you didn't love me" came out in a whisper.

He hauled her over to him. "I left because I loved you too much to make you sit and watch me wallow until I pulled myself together. I wasn't sure I could after what had happened overseas."

She blinked up at him, her amber eyes reaching deep inside him. She was the only one who'd affected him like that. Damn that she looked sexy and vulnerable. Did it mean something that she still wore his old AC/DC T-shirt to bed?

She pushed off him and sat up. "Isn't that what families do? They stick around and help each other through rough patches. They don't walk out when things get tough. They stay together and work through problems."

"I already apologized. I don't know what else to say about it." There was no way to make her understand. Luke had always had to be tough. Especially after his father had ditched the family. His eldest brother, Nick, had carried most of the burden. Luke had pulled his own weight, doing whatever was necessary to protect their tight-knit family. One thing he hadn't done was dump his problems on others.

Campbell boys held their own.

"Walking out on someone who loves you is just cruel."

The sadness and pain in her voice almost doubled him over. She folded her arms and gripped her elbows.

True. But walking away was still better than dragging her to the depths of hell alongside him. He still hadn't completely healed.

Before he could say anything else, she climbed off the bed and grabbed her clothes.

He didn't want to be selfish when it came to Julie. It hurt seeing her like this, but maybe it was best if they kept a little distance between them over the next few days or weeks until they wrapped this case.

Maybe the two of them together wasn't such a good thing. He had options. There were safe houses...

Luke's cell buzzed.

He picked up his phone and checked the text.

There was a picture of him and Julie on her steps from last night. His arm was around her. The photo was captioned Hope you enjoy watching her die.

Rob had been there.

Right now, Luke wouldn't have been able to think clearly if he couldn't see for himself that she was safe. Could he be there for her, protect her, and keep his heart out of it?

No choice.

Ravishing Rob wasn't forgiving. He'd set his sights on Julie.

Luke would do whatever it took to make sure Rob failed. Besides, rushing into another killing wasn't his typical style. Normally, he worked on his "projects" for weeks, sometimes months. Mistakes happened when people got in a hurry.

Could he make a slip?

Luke hoped so. He'd be right there to make the arrest. If he could get five minutes alone with the lowlife, Luke would gladly check his badge and gun at the door. Rob wouldn't be anyone's problem once Luke was finished.

The guy was thorough. And he wouldn't stop until he had Julie's head.

Literally.

# Chapter Five

"Were you on a call?" Julie walked into the master bed-room dressed and ready to go wearing a pair of jeans, beige boots and a cream-colored pullover sweater.

Luke stood near the bed. He had his hand in his pocket as he stared out the window. From his profile she could see that all color had drained from his face.

"What's wrong?" She froze.

"Had to update my boss."

"Everything okay?"

"Fine." He'd dressed in jeans and a black T-shirt. His muscles stretched and thinned as he walked toward her. The fabric pulled taut across his thighs as they flexed. He was the perfect mix of athleticism and grace.

"You're sure?" She stepped aside to let him pass.

"'Course," he said, and his voice was stiff. Hurt?

How many times had she begged him to tell her what was going on before? He'd refused. And yet, this time he'd been different. He'd opened up to her a little and allowed her a peek inside. The idea of a friendship had seemed possible. So, what had suddenly changed?

All she wanted was an update on the case. What had his boss said?

Once again, Luke was holding back. Not letting her in. As much as she wanted to believe otherwise, nothing was different. Sure, he'd opened up a little. Her and Luke's relationship, trust, had inched forward. So, why was he reverting to his old ways? She could tell that whatever had gone down with his boss a few minutes ago was important.

What was that saying about teaching old dogs?

Luke's trick was to shut her out when he got emotional.

"Do you have eggs?" she asked, resigned.

He nodded as she followed him downstairs.

"We need to move to a safe house as quickly as possible." He stopped on the staircase and cocked his head sideways.

"Why can't we just stay here?" She wished they could plant themselves somewhere. His place was comfortable, and even though she didn't have anything here that belonged to her, oddly it felt like home. Their old town house had been foreign to her ever since he'd left. And yet, she couldn't bring herself to sell.

"I'm afraid not. It was late last night, so this was our best bet for sleep. I don't want to push it, though."

The wooden floors creaked downstairs.

Luke pulled his gun. His cell vibrated. He fished it out of his pocket and checked the screen.

A furtive glance toward her, followed by a narrowed gaze focused on the bottom of the stairwell, and Julie knew something bad was about to happen.

"What did it say?" she whispered.

His movement slowed and became purposeful as he wedged himself in front of her and downstairs.

She put her hand on his shoulder. "Luke. Don't shut me out again."

He handed her his phone.

The text read Come down and make breakfast for all of us. I'm here. And that bitch you're with is one step closer to getting what she deserves.

Luke took his cell from her, peeling back her white-knuckle grip slowly. He fired off several texts before easing down the stairs, weapon drawn, motioning Julie to stay behind him.

She had every intention of being glue.

A knock at the front door made her jump.

Shuffling noises were heard as Luke hopped the last couple of stairs and rounded the corner.

Julie followed. The place looked clear, save for the back door being left open.

The doorbell rang several times.

Luke closed and locked the back door after checking the powder room and announcing, "Clear."

He moved to the front door and to a waiting officer, holding his badge in full view as he opened the door.

The officer greeted him and asked permission to come inside.

Luke nodded. They swept the area one more time for safety's sake as more squad cars arrived out front.

"Anything out of place, sir?"

"No. He managed to disarm my alarm, though, and leave out the back door before I could catch him."

"I'll write a report," the officer said. He spoke into his radio then turned his attention to Luke.

"You didn't see anything outside?"

"No, sir. I heard a noise around the side of the house, called it in and vacated my post to investigate. Everything looked fine."

"The noise must've spooked him." He thanked the officer and let him out, locking the door behind him.

"How'd he get inside?" She repressed the fear nipping at her.

"A skilled burglar can bypass even the best alarm systems. There will be more police protection around this place than we need for the next few hours, but it'll be safe for now."

Julie followed Luke as he moved toward the kitchen, reminding herself to breathe through her stress.

His broad back and strong shoulders were eye level as he walked in front of her. Did he know how difficult it was not to reach out to touch him? Get lost in him? Let him be her strength?

But she'd touched that stove once.

Had the burn marks to prove it.

Wasn't the definition of insanity repeating the same mistake over and over again but expecting a different result?

Besides, seeing the man who'd lit wildfires inside her brought back all sorts of raging memories. And the very real disappointment that he'd been her only failure. Luke had been her biggest regret. And that was playing tricks on her emotions. She'd been ready to move on before. Hadn't she?

Luke stopped and she bumped into his back. God help her, but it was like walking into a brick wall with a much better view. "Sorry about that. Wasn't paying attention. Step aside. I'm sure I can whip something up. What have you got in here other than eggs?"

She moved beside him and glanced around the kitchen.

"Sit." He pointed to a bar stool on the other side of the bar.

"What? You? Cook?"

"Try not to look so surprised."

The corners of his mouth turned up in a sexy little grin. His eyes told a different story. An emotion she couldn't quite put her finger on flickered behind his brown gaze. Worry? Fear?

"Okay. Fine. Let me see what you can do, big man."
She perched on the seat.

Not five minutes later, she had a steaming cup of coffee in her hand. "Thank you, Mr. Campbell."

When she smiled after taking a sip, he shot her an I-told-you-so look.

She rolled her eyes. "Of course you can brew a pot. It's good. But I'm still waiting to be impressed with your culinary skills."

After experiencing his handiwork with an iron skillet, a handful of eggs and chopped veggies, she was too full to eat her words.

She put her hands up in the universal sign of surrender. "Okay. You got me. Where'd you learn to cook like that?"

"My sisters taught me. What can I say, I missed your cooking." He pulled a seat across the island from her and sat down with his own plate. "You really like it?"

"Not bad, Campbell." She leaned back in her seat and folded her arms after swallowing the last bite. Not wanting to get too comfortable in his home, she added, "Where are we heading today?"

"The first two stops are Addison and Dallas. We find something there, and we save ourselves a driving tour of Texas. Just give me a minute to finish eating and throw together an overnight bag. And you should bring your stuff, too. If we hit a dead end around here, we'll head to Austin next."

"Live-music capital of the world." Was he thinking the same thing she was? Their first weekend trip together had been to watch the bats under the Congress Avenue Bridge at sunset.

He nodded, picking up his plate.

"The least I can do is clean the dishes." She moved around the island to where he stood.

Luke didn't immediately move. Nor did she.

The air charged around them, electrified with sexual chemistry. She couldn't deny missing Luke. Or thinking about him. She'd dreamed about him more than she cared to admit in the past few years.

She cleared her dry throat.

He hesitated, then half smiled and walked away.

Was he thinking about all the times they'd abandoned breakfast dishes and made love on the kitchen counter? The island?

She could almost feel his strong hands around her hips, helping her move with him as he thrust deeper and deeper home.

Julie shook off the memory and turned on the faucet, trying not to think about the changes in Luke as she loaded the dishwasher.

He logged on to his laptop. His solemn expression had returned. "The crime scene was clear except for a print in the yard. The team's running analysis on the type of shoe to see if we can find anything there."

"Doesn't sound like they have much to work with."

"Unfortunately, no. I'd hoped for more this time around." He stood and motioned toward the garage door. "The print is unusual. Might give us something else to go on."

Julie followed him and buckled in. "How many people has he…?"

"Six so far."

"All women?" she asked, but figured she already knew the answer.

"Yes."

"And what he did to her…to my client… Does he do that to all his victims?"

"Pretty much." Luke backed out of the garage, watching every movement around them. "Usually worse."

He cut their heads off? A rock sat in Julie's stomach.

She sat quietly for the rest of the twenty-minute drive. As usual, I-635 was a parking lot, gearing up for the lunch rush.

He exited onto the Dallas North Tollway, then took Beltline to Addison Road. "The first name on the list lives on Quorum Drive."

"I remember when these apartments were being built. Thought this area was for young professionals."

"Our guy is smart. Profile says he's probably educated and most likely in his early thirties."

A chill gripped her spine. "Sounds like the kind of person I could walk down the street next to and never realize he's a monster."

"That's what makes guys like him so hard to track. We catch killers with a low IQ quickly."

"So, he could be young, attractive and rich?"

"Yes."

"Then why? Why would someone who has it all need to do…that…to women? Is he crazy?"

"No. Believe it or not, he's not crazy. To people like you and me he seems that way. His actions are calculated, justified in his twisted mind. This guy enjoys researching 'projects,' as he calls them. Once he identifies his mark, he studies her. Learns her daily patterns. We have at least two cases where we know he hacked into their computers."

"Doesn't that leave a cybertrail?"

"He's not stupid. Every IP we follow leads us to a dead end. So far, he's been a step ahead. But he's arrogant."

"With me, in my case, it's different. Isn't it? I wasn't on his radar before."

"No."

She sucked in a burst of air. "Then why me?"

"You fit his M.O. He targets women between the ages

of twenty-five to twenty-seven with black hair. Plus, you may have seen him and you're connected to me." Luke's hand covered hers. "He'll make a mistake and we'll be right there to catch him. He doesn't normally work like this, and that's a good thing. He's moving too fast. I'm not going to let him get to you. That's why you're here with me. I'm keeping you right by my side, where I can watch you at all times."

"I'm glad it's you and not some stranger." She smiled weakly. "No way would someone else care this much."

Guilt or whatever it was that made Luke want to give her life back didn't matter. Her safety in exchange for him being able to walk away with a clean conscience didn't seem like a bad trade.

But could she really trust him? He wasn't the first person who'd been emotionally unavailable. Hadn't her father primed her for men like Luke? Except that she'd believed he was different, had broken all her rules for him, and then he'd shut her out just like her father always had.

Freud would've had a field day.

A little piece of her protested, saying that Luke had been different. The part of her that wanted to believe in him no matter what logical evidence was presented against it. But then, emotions weren't ruled by reason.

Luke pulled into an off-street parking spot and cut the ignition. He double-checked the address on his phone. "Stick behind me."

She did.

Being with Luke brought a dangerous sense of comfort.

LUKE HELD THE door open and waited for Julie to climb out of the cab. She deserved to know what she was up against, so he'd shared case information. Her reaction left him wondering if that had been such a good idea. The part about Luke fearing for her life he'd keep close to his chest.

Luke's hands fisted.

The deranged jerk wouldn't get to her. Not as long as Luke was alive. Period.

Intel said the person in this building wasn't likely the one Luke was searching for. Chad Devel was twenty-six years old. He worked as a sous chef in a nearby trendy restaurant and had had three loud-music complaints at this address in the past six months. He'd been pulled over twice and hauled in for suspicion of driving while intoxicated. He'd pleaded out once. The other DWI case was pending.

Not exactly the kind of guy concerned with flying under the radar.

"Which building?" Julie asked. Her voice still sounded sweet to him, like waking up late on a Saturday morning in a cabin in the woods.

A quick glance at his phone and he pointed to the one on the right. "We're looking for apartment number one hundred fifty."

He'd spotted it as he'd said it. "There. Ground floor."

"Looks pricey."

"Would take someone with a good job to afford a place like this."

"Maybe even with a college degree?" She looked at him intently with those amber eyes. "Do sous chefs normally have degrees?"

"Sometimes." Luke palmed his badge and knocked on the door. Since Chad seemed to enjoy partying at night, he'd most likely still be asleep.

No one answered.

The next knocks sounded off louder, more urgently. "Mr. Devel. Open up."

"Okay, okay" came through the door.

It swung open.

A young guy with curly hair stood at the opened door. He blinked against the bright sun and shielded his eyes with his forearm. His gaze moved from Luke to Julie. "What do you want?"

"Are you Chad Devel?"

The young guy looked as if he'd just stepped out of an Abercrombie & Fitch commercial. He had on boxer shorts and no shirt. He was tall, at least six feet, with a lean runner's build. His sandy-blond hair looked windswept, as if he'd just gotten off a yacht. He rubbed his blue eyes and bit back a yawn.

Luke flashed his badge. "I'm Special Agent Campbell. May we come in?"

Surprise widened the young guy's gaze as he stood there stunned. Typical reaction.

"You didn't answer either of my questions."

"Oh. Right. Yes, I'm Chad. I haven't done anything wrong. My court date isn't until—"

"Where were you the night before last, Mr. Devel?" On first appraisal, this kid looked as though he'd grown up with too much money and free time. Yet, he had a job. Maybe Daddy had cut him off?

"Work."

Easy enough to verify. "And that is where?"

"DeBleu on Beltline close to Midway. Why?"

"May we come inside?" Luke asked again. He'd like the chance to look around. Make certain he didn't need to circle back to this guy later.

"Um, sure." The door swung open wide. "The place is a mess. Had a few friends over last night after work."

Luke stepped inside, motioning Julie to follow. "Can your boss corroborate your story?"

"Yeah. He was there. I worked with Tony and Angie, too. They can tell you where I was. They were here last night. I can give you their phone numbers if you want to check."

Luke pulled out his phone and took the information. The guy didn't fit the profile for Rob, but Luke didn't plan on taking any chances with this case.

Besides, something about Chad had Luke's radar up.

Chad's heartbeat at the base of his throat beat too rapidly. Not exactly probable cause for an arrest, but Luke didn't like it. He'd lean on him a little bit. See if he could fish any information out. He handed Chad a piece of paper and a pen. "Write your name."

He complied.

Luke studied the page. The handwriting didn't match Rob's note, which could be on purpose. Most serial killers didn't warn their victims in advance. Rob was no exception. This was all a big game to the bastard. "Where'd you go to college?"

"Here, locally. Dropped out after a couple semesters."

"Your dad work in the medical field?"

"No."

"What did you study?"

Chad's dark eyebrows knitted. "Finance. Why?"

The apartment was small but upscale. Luke could see to the back door from where he stood in the living room. There were hardwood floors, contemporary furnishings. Ansel Adams black-and-white photos hung on the walls. There were no signs of the souvenirs Rob liked to take from his victims, but that didn't mean he would keep them at his house or out in the open. Empty imported-beer bottles lined the glass coffee table. Sofa cushions were strewn around. "Looks like you had a good time."

"We did. Didn't get much sleep." Chad's gaze darted around.

Half of an unrolled cigar lay open on the glass coffee table, a common place to hide weed. Pot was small-time compared to what Luke was used to seeing. Could Chad be on heavy drugs? K2?

Possibly.

Three years on the job had Luke's interest piqued. While he wasn't there to pop the guy for a nickel bag, Luke didn't plan to share.

Chad needed to sweat, and by the looks of him, he was.

Luke moved to the coffee table, picked up the cigar and rolled it under his nose. "Cuban?"

"No, sir. Those are illegal. That one's from Venezuela." Chad shifted his weight to his other foot. A few seconds later, he did it again.

Luke focused on Chad.

"You like to hunt?"

"Not really. My dad forces us to go on a trip once a year." Chad kept chancing a look toward Julie. Luke didn't like the way Chad looked at her. Then again, after Rob's direct threat this morning, Luke was on high alert.

"Your dad live around here?"

"No, sir. California."

There was another point worth considering. Rob knew what Julie looked like. Chad didn't have a clue when he saw her. Luke had been careful to gauge the guy's reaction to her. There would have been some hint of recognition. Pupils dilated. A twitch.

Chad hadn't so much as lifted a thick brow. "You have any medical conditions?"

"No, sir. Why?"

"You don't take medicine?"

"No."

"Mind if I check your cabinets?"

"Go ahead."

Luke motioned for Julie to stay by the door as he moved to the open-concept kitchen and flipped through cabinets and drawers. No medicine bottles or telltale syringes were present. The bathroom was across the living room. The door was open to the main space. He checked the medicine chest before returning.

"Do you have any relatives in the area?"

"My mom lives in Dallas."

"That it?"

"Yeah...um...no. Wait a minute. I have a half brother, if he counts. My parents divorced when I was a kid. My dad moved out of state with his second wife. They had a kid. Got a text from him last month saying he'd moved here."

Chad's age pushed the boundaries of Rob's profile. His half brother would be even younger. "Must be nice to have family in town."

"Not really. We aren't close. He's flaky."

"That's tough when families split. You two didn't grow up together?"

Chad nearly choked. "Not on my mother's life would she stand for that."

"How come?"

"This woman and my dad had been having an affair since before I was born. Rick, my half brother, is four years older than me."

This put him at the exact age of the profile, which meant nothing if the guy was in California the whole time. Julie's eyes widened. She caught on to it, too.

If the brother had just moved here, he wouldn't show up in any databases yet. "Those hunting trips you mentioned."

"Yeah?"

"Your brother into them?"

"He likes them a hell of a lot more than I do. Why?"

"Do you have contact information for Rick? I'd like to speak to him."

"Um, yeah. I think. It would be on my phone. Hold on." Chad moved to the bar separating the living space from the kitchen and started shifting stacks of junk. Mail, papers, books were tossed around.

Couch cushions were next. He checked behind each one. "Oh, wait. I know where it is."

Chad disappeared into the bathroom, returning a moment later holding up a pair of jeans. He fished in the front pocket and produced his cell. Another few seconds of scrolling through text messages and he stopped on a name. He tilted the screen toward Luke. The name read Rick Camden.

"That's your half brother?"

"Yeah." Chad rolled his eyes and tossed his hair back. "His mom didn't want to give them away by naming him after my father. Turns out, the sleazy bitch worked at my dad's office."

"You have an address?"

"No. Sorry. I haven't even seen him."

The women Rob chose were between the ages of twenty-five and twenty-seven. All had black hair. Had Dad's sleeping around caused Chad or his mother to resent women?

Interesting theory. Luke made a mental note to check into Chad's mother's background, too. Female serial killers might be rare, but the few who crossed the line were vicious. Time to find out if the bloodline could use some bleach.

Of course, that didn't explain the male voice who'd phoned Luke before. Although, she might be *that* crafty. "Doesn't sound like the family recovered once their secret came out in the open." Luke could relate to the bitterness he saw in Chad's eyes at his father's abandonment. He also knew that holding on to anger was like drinking poison and expecting it to kill someone else.

Chad shook his head. "We don't exactly get together for holidays."

Luke took note of Rick's information. "This guy grew up in California?"

"Uh-huh."

The way Rob studied his intended victims didn't mesh logistically with someone who lived out of state. But with money like theirs, he could travel back and forth. Even so, Luke would follow up. He'd become the best because he was thorough.

"What about your brother?"

"Half brother," Chad corrected.

"Sorry. He have any medical conditions you know about?"

"Nah. Not to my knowledge. But then, I wouldn't really know."

"You look like your mom or your dad?"

"My mom."

"You have a picture of her?" He needed to see if Chad's mother had black hair.

Chad produced a photo on his cell phone. The image of him and his mother showed their family resemblance.

"What about Rick's mom? She still alive?"

"Yeah. She's pretty, I guess. She's thin. Has black hair."

Interviewing Rick just became a priority.

"We'll be in contact should we have any more questions," Luke said as he made a move toward the door.

"Can you tell me what this is about, at least?"

"Murder." Luke let the word hang in the air.

The guy shook as if he might unravel. Rob was so detached he'd most likely be calm, no matter what. He didn't see what he did to women as bad. In his eyes, killing them was justified.

"Look, I'm not perfect. I like to party. But I would never hurt anyone on purpose."

With his tanned face and Kennedy family–like good looks, Luke figured it wouldn't be hard to find women who wanted to party with Chad.

"Keep it that way," he said as he opened the door for Julie.

One down. Seven to go. Rick was a better fit to the profile. Too bad he hadn't lived in Texas over the past two years.

"I will, sir."

Based on the guy's fearful expression, he wouldn't be so much as jaywalking anytime soon. Chad knew how to throw a party. Was he a killer?

Luke followed Julie back to the truck with the ever-present feeling of eyes on them. He matched her stride and possessively put his hand low on her back.

A visual scan revealed nothing suspect. Chad's door was closed.

So, what was with the creepy feeling?

# Chapter Six

Julie wasn't sure what to expect if she saw a killer face-to-face. Would she even know?

"You were tense in there," she said to Luke on the short walk to the truck.

"I don't like his half brother. I can't ignore the link to the Devel name. His age matches the profile. He likes to hunt. His mother has black hair. We'll know more once we talk to him." He paused for a couple of beats. "The only problem is, the killings are happening in the Dallas–Fort Worth Metroplex, and he's supposedly been in California."

She climbed into the cab of the truck and clicked on her seat belt. "Chad said his half brother doesn't have any medical problems. Isn't your guy supposed to be a diabetic?"

"Could be. Then again, he might've just been thirsty." She had picked up on that. Luke's fingers gripped the steering wheel so tightly, they turned white.

He palmed his cell and punched in Rick's number.

"Interesting."

"What is it?"

"The number's bad. It's been disconnected."

"Does that mean he left town? His brother said he wasn't stable."

"Could be. I'll have Nick check into it." He sent a text

to his brother asking for any information he could dig up about Rick Camden. "Or Chad gave us a fake number."

"He seemed like a typical twenty-year-old to me." She shrugged. "If it turns out he's the killer, I wouldn't be any good at your job."

"He could hold a grudge against his stepmother for ruining his family. Some serial killers are charming and popular, and they can start at any age."

"Oh." That last bit of information sat hard on her stomach. "He was good-looking. A woman might never know who she was dealing with until it was too late."

"That's Rob's M.O." Luke started the engine, pulled out of the parking lot and made his way back onto the Tollway.

"So he calls himself Ravishing Rob?"

"Captivates then decapitates."

A wave of nausea slammed into her as Ms. Martin's face flashed through her mind. Julie bent forward to stave off the bile rising in her throat. She'd stopped him from cutting off her client's head, which hardly seemed like a consolation under the circumstances. And now he wanted hers. "What kind of monster does that to people?"

"I'm sorry. That was too much information."

She dragged in a breath. "No. It's good. I need to hear everything. Believe me, there are moments when I just don't want to know. But I have to be prepared, right?"

"Yes, but you can do this in doses. If this is more than you can handle, I can drop you at the station during the day while I investigate. You'll be safe there."

How did she tell him there was nowhere she'd rather be than with him? That she only felt truly safe by his side? "No. I'm fine. I knew this would be hard. I have to toughen up and stay informed. This might be difficult, but it's important, and I can't close myself off to all the bad things in the world. That could get me killed someday. Plus, what if you don't get back tonight? Where would that leave me?"

"Right now, let's think about something else." His gaze stayed focused on the road in front of him as he moved the pickup through traffic.

"I like it when you include me. I mean, you didn't for so long. This is a lot to process, believe me, but I'd rather know."

"And I'd rather protect you from the truth." His tone was solemn. Regret?

Did he mean now or before? Both?

"Can I ask a question?"

He nodded.

"What happened to you in Iraq?"

"War." His gaze intensified on the stretch of road in front of him. His hands gripped the wheel tighter.

"I know you went overseas, but I mean, you didn't talk about it when you came home. The guys you served with were like brothers…"

His nod was almost imperceptible.

Whatever happened must've been pretty bad. After all these years, he still couldn't talk about it. Not even after all they'd been through in the past twenty-four hours. Maybe he would never be able to share. "Whatever it was, I'm sorry."

"I hope you don't think any of what happened between us was your fault."

"It takes two people to wreck a marriage."

"No. It doesn't. It takes two people to make a good marriage. Only one to destroy it."

"If only I'd—"

He pulled the truck off the Tollway and into a hotel parking lot where he parked.

The force of his stare when he turned to face her threw her.

"Believe me when I say you did nothing wrong."

Hot tears of frustration pricked the backs of her eyes. "If that were true, we'd still be married and none of this would be happening."

"I repeat, none of what happened to us was your fault." The intensity of his gaze matched the determination in his clenched jaw.

The words were like bullets through her heart. No matter what he said, it wouldn't change the fact she was a failure. Her father had drilled it into her head that Davises didn't give up. Yet, she had. "How can you say that? It takes two people to kill a relationship, Luke. If I'd been a better wife, you would've been able to confide in me. You wouldn't have walked out."

"I take full responsibility."

"They teach you that in counseling? That it was all your fault?"

"No" came out through thinned lips.

"Why, Luke? Why'd you walk out?" Her emotions were taking over, and she knew she shouldn't ask the question. But she had. Well, she'd said it. Couldn't take her words back now. Everything happening around her made her realize just how fragile life really was. One minute, she thought she was starting to figure out her next move and get comfortable in life, and then everything changed just like before.

"Because I was broken, dammit. I came back damaged. They were killed. All of them." He hung his head low.

The truth crushed down on her rib cage, making it hurt to even breathe. Based on his expression, he seemed as devastated as she felt.

"We were ambushed."

Her heart ached for him. She couldn't imagine what that would do to a person. And yet a little piece of her heart filled with hope. He was finally talking about the past. Telling her something important.

"It was my fault."

She put her hand on his arm, ignoring the pulses of electricity she'd come to expect whenever they touched. "Couldn't have been."

He got quiet.

"I wish I could've been there for you, Luke." She couldn't stop the sieve now that it had opened.

"You were perfect. I wasn't. It was my fault. Everything. I hurt you and I couldn't keep going like that. You didn't deserve to be treated like that."

"I was expendable. You must've realized we'd made a mistake. You didn't want me anymore. You left." Tears streamed down her cheeks.

He brought his hand up and brushed them away, only glancing over at her for a second then quickly shifting back to the empty parking spot in front of them. "Do you want to know how much I wanted you back then? How much I still want you?"

She nodded.

His gaze met hers as the space between them disappeared faster than she could blink.

He leaned into her and kissed her, hard, bruising, hungry.

LUKE EXPECTED JULIE to pull back or push him away. Slap him. She didn't.

When her hands came up and her fingers tunneled into his hair, urging him even closer, he battled every instinct he had to lay the seat down and unleash all the primal instincts that had built up in the years since he'd been gone. He was already hard.

He deepened the kiss. She tasted like honey and coffee with just a little bit of spearmint left over from brushing her teeth this morning.

Her lips moved against his, and he swallowed her soft moan. Awareness zinged through his body, wiring his muscles even tighter.

He thrust his tongue in her mouth, and she met his every stroke.

A niggle of conscience ate at his gut.

Her nerves were fried. She'd been through hell. She was reaching out to him for comfort…and he was crossing the line.

Oh, hell. This was one of those rare times he wished he could set aside what was right for what was right *now*.

The hurt expression on her face a few minutes ago would haunt his dreams.

He shivered then pulled back. "I can't do this."

The back of her hand came up to her swollen, pink lips. Her breathing was heavy but she didn't speak. Her gaze trained out the window ahead of her, as though she was trying to make sense of…this.

He hated hurting her again.

What was broken in him that made him assume everyone would turn their backs on him eventually?

His father?

Luke couldn't deny having his old man walk out before Luke was old enough to say the guy's name had damaged him. His family tree left leaves of betrayal scattered around the earth, which only proved to Luke that he couldn't trust his instincts when it came to love.

Then there was his first love, Chloe. The day she'd bolted was still fresh in his mind. The conversation as vivid today as it had been when they'd had it. With no money to go to college, he'd decided to join the military first. Believing what he had with Chloe was real, he'd shared his plans to save money so they could get married someday. But first, he needed to help his family get out of debt.

She didn't respond well to the fact he needed to help out back home, saying she'd expected to come first in his life. That she'd pouted had caught him off guard.

Chloe demanded he change his plans and join her at the state school she'd planned to attend in the fall. Her look of disappointment when he'd balked was still stamped in Luke's mind. An only child to wealthy parents, Chloe was used to getting everything her way.

But Luke had responsibilities. Commitments. His family had been everything to him and there was no way he'd turn his back on them.

When she couldn't convince him otherwise, she broke it off, but not before she let him know just how much he'd hurt her.

Deep down, he'd realized what he'd had with her was puppy love. Yet, it didn't stop him from licking his wounds from her betrayal or closing off another little piece of his heart to the world.

Didn't people always bolt when life got serious?

It wasn't that much longer after that when he'd met Julie, fallen hard and figured out what real love was. He'd been able to trust it while times were good. But when he came home a mess and saw disappointment in her eyes…he'd assumed she'd do what everyone else had. Walk away.

He'd preempted.

Ringtones broke through his heavy thoughts. He pulled out his cell and checked the screen. His brother Nick was calling. Good. "Did you find anything for me on those background checks?"

"Nothing helpful, I'm afraid. Most of the men on the list are too old. None had medical issues. The only person who comes close to fitting is Chad Devel, who doesn't fit your profile."

"Just left his place. Did you find anything on his half brother?"

"Nothing yet."

"His brother said he just moved to the area a month ago from California."

"And he has no idea where he lives?"

"That's what he says. Doesn't seem to be any love lost between them. The family was split by an affair. Get this—Rick's mother has black hair."

"Not exactly a saw with blood on it."

"True. I'll take any lead I can get in this case," he said wearily. "Dig around a little? See what you come up with? And will you check into his mother, too?"

"Will do. I'll be in touch."

Luke ended the call as Julie touched his arm. "What were you thinking about before?"

"Nothing," he lied, glancing around to get his bearings and register his thoughts firmly in the present. He'd hoped for something interesting to come out of the background checks. He repositioned as he scanned the area, careful to watch for anyone who might be trying to surprise them, ignoring the heat radiating up his arm from her touch. Satisfied they were safe, he settled into his seat and rubbed the scruff on his chin. "I came back a mess. You know that already. What you didn't know is that I was a POW."

"I'm so sorry, Luke." Tears brimmed in her eyes.

An overwhelming urge to lean over and capture those pink lips again assaulted him. As much as he wanted to kiss away her tears, hear her say his name over and over again when she hit the heights of sexual desire, he refused to let his hormones rule. "Beatings and starvation were a couple of their favorite forms of torture. But that just scratched the surface. They saved the worst for later."

And now she knew more than his family and the U.S. government put together. Could he tell her the rest even if he wanted to? He doubted it.

Thinking about it shot his anger level to red-hot alert. The psychiatrist had pushed him to open up and discuss his time in enemy camp. He couldn't. Not even with a trained professional. This was different. He felt less exposed with Julie.

"Did all this have anything to do with the award you hid?"

"You found that?" There'd never been any mention of it before. But then, he hadn't exactly been easy to talk to back then.

She nodded. "I didn't open it, though. I promise."

"Didn't feel like I deserved a medal for living."

Her amber eyes filled with remorse and tears and maybe just a little bit of hope.

There was no fantasy she'd take him back. And yet, for whatever crazy reason, a little piece of the armor he'd secured around his heart cracked.

"You're a survivor, Luke. Not many people can say that."

"No one deserves a medal because they kept breathing." Or for not being there for his squad when they needed him. For all intents and purposes, he'd abandoned them. Just like his own father had abandoned him. How could he live with himself? He'd lived the pain firsthand, so to inflict it on others, willingly or not, was more than he could bear.

She paused, her forehead wrinkling in the way it did when she was concentrating. "You came back so thin. And you'd stopped talking to everyone. Me, your family. You changed so much I almost didn't recognize you."

"There was nothing but anger and hurt inside me. I wanted to lash out. Fight something. Except, there you were. You represented everything good in my life. One look and I knew I didn't deserve you—would never be good enough for you."

He expected anger when he glanced at her to see if there was any possibility she could understand where he was coming from. In Luke's life, he'd learned when things got tough, people left. Instead, Julie gave him compassion.

"That's just not true, Luke. You didn't have to go through that alone."

She touched his hand. Electricity and warmth moved through him, spreading from the point of contact.

Julie. *His Julie.*

He'd asked himself a thousand times what he'd done to deserve her. Even for the short time she'd belonged to him. Never could come up with an answer.

"I didn't know how to open up. Not exactly a Campbell trait. We held our family together by taking care of things, not by moving our mouths."

"I remember how worried they were about you. Especially Gran."

"I got through it eventually." Problem was, when he came up on the other side of that dark hole he'd been in, Julie was gone. He'd pushed her away and didn't have the first idea of how to get her back. Didn't figure he could. He assumed most ships that sailed didn't come back to shore. "For what it's worth, I'm sorry."

"I know."

Luke scanned the lot. His gaze stopped at a sedan parked under the hotel canopy.

"Everything okay?"

He shot a glance toward Julie. Her brow was arched, her forehead wrinkled.

"Not sure yet."

The tension radiating from her body filled the air thickly, but she held her head high.

Why did that make him proud? He had no right to feel anything when it came to Julie.

Tell that to his body. To his heart.

He put the gearshift in Drive and eased toward the car. As he neared, the gray sedan snaked between several cars and sped off. Luke tried to navigate in the same traffic but his truck was too big.

"That car?" She pointed to the sedan.

"Yeah. There's something not right. I can feel it. Let's check it out." He put his pickup in Reverse and made a big circle around the check-in lane under the canopy of the grand hotel.

The car was gone.

Luke hooked a right turn out of the parking lot. People in a hurry didn't wait for lights to change green. They always turned right, and this guy had been in a rush.

A phone call to his boss about Rick and his mother would have to wait. Garcia needed an update, too. Luke made a mental note to do it later and moved on while he scanned vehicles.

Julie's quiet demeanor told him all he needed to know about how she was processing the events. When she was truly scared, she got real still. Fear or not, she never backed down. It was one of the many qualities he admired about her.

Two more right turns and he was on the service road to the Tollway. If the guy hit the on-ramp, it'd be all over. He could disappear into the myriad cars snaking down the road.

If Luke had been able to see a license plate, even a partial, he could call Detective Garcia and have the jerk's home address in ten minutes or less.

"There. Over there. Do you see him?" Julie's voice rose in a mix of adrenaline and fear. "Is that him?"

Luke maneuvered closer to the gray sedan. His left hand was planted firmly on the steering wheel, his right gripping his weapon. "Might be. Let's get a closer look."

The car made a quick left before he could get a visual on the driver.

At least half a dozen cars separated them.

Luke swerved in traffic and sped up. An SUV blocked his view.

Horns honked as he pushed in between cars and cut off others. "If you get a good visual, call out the license plate."

"Okay." Julie pulled her cell from her purse and repositioned in her seat, craning her neck to get a better look.

She had to be scared half to death. The sedan stayed in sight just enough to keep Luke on its tail. Although he'd love to get the license plate, it could be a fake. Whoever was driving seemed to know what he was doing, which brought him back to a point he hadn't wanted to consider but had been eating at the back of his mind all day. The killer had uncanny access to information, which he knew how to use. Another troublesome fact: the man sure knew how to hunt someone.

Even though Rick Camden was an interesting lead, Luke had to consider other possibilities, including the unthinkable. Could Rob work in law enforcement? The officer who'd appeared on the scene first at Julie's town house had disappeared a little too quickly. Was it possible that Luke stared Rob in the face and didn't know it? There had been no sirens, no squad car.

Had Rob gotten away with the crime he'd committed in the alley because he wore a uniform? A chill gripped Luke's spine.

A law-enforcement officer going rogue was one of the

worst possible scenarios. A man trained to kill wasn't a good person to have hunting Julie.

Of course, the guy wouldn't have to be currently on the force. He could be disgruntled, disillusioned, or might have been kicked off. Another possibility was that he might've flunked out of the academy and enjoyed playing cop. Of course, the more likely scenario involved someone who worked in the medical field. Even so, Luke didn't want to rule anything out.

The bastard had somehow gotten Luke's home address. He already had his cell number.

What else did Rob know?

## Chapter Seven

"He's gone." Luke sighed sharply. The car he'd been following had disappeared.

"I wish I could've gotten at least a partial plate." Julie gripped her seat belt where it crossed her chest and leaned against the headrest. She sat silent for a long moment. Her forehead creased the way it did when she was concentrating, and her lips compressed into a thin line.

He could tell she was having trouble processing what had just happened. She needed a distraction. "We should think about eating lunch."

"How about that barbecue place at Preston and LBJ?" She blinked her eyes open.

How could he forget? It was their favorite. "Sounds good. Let's check it out."

"Luke."

"Yeah."

"Thanks for telling me what you did in the parking lot before. It helps."

"It was true." Their earlier conversation, being able to tell her that everything had been his fault, had lightened what otherwise would've been a horrendous mood on a screwed-up day. And that shocked him.

Wasn't like him to get all talky and share his feelings with anyone. Even more surprising was that he'd felt better afterward. As if the boulder that had been sitting on his chest since he'd left Julie had dislodged. Still there, but less pressure weighing down on him. Not much else was going his way today and he sure didn't like the feeling of always chasing behind Rob. The coldhearted killer was always a step ahead. Bright guy.

But that she'd believed she was a failure because of their broken marriage pierced right through him. None of it had been her fault. For what it was worth, he'd go back and change everything if he could. But life didn't give do-overs. Luke figured all he could do was move forward and not repeat his mistakes.

Within ten minutes, he'd parked in the busy lot. "Doesn't look like they're hurting for business."

"Nope."

He opened Julie's door and then followed her inside. They got in line and stood in silence, contemplating the menu. After all that had happened, he was glad she had an appetite at all.

Julie took in a deep breath. "I haven't been here in a long time. Still smells the same."

The Barbecue Shack brought back a flood of good memories. "Just like Sunday afternoons at Gran's ranch."

"My mouth is already watering." She turned to face him, smiling. "You guys used to smoke a brisket in the slow cooker all day."

"The food was ready when the sun kissed the horizon."

"Remember all those evenings in the barn after supper?" Her cheeks flushed a soft pink.

"Some of the best nights of my life."

"You come here a lot? You know, since we…"

"No. Not since us."

He put his hand on the small of her back, urging her as

the line moved forward. Touching Julie felt as natural as waking up in the morning.

Nothing in his world had been right in a long time.

"Being here, together, seems a lot like old times, doesn't it?" She turned and pushed up on her tiptoes, planting a kiss on his cheek.

Blood roared in his ears and his heartbeat thundered in his chest. "Yeah. It's nice."

"I like being friends, Luke." Her gaze lingered on his.

"Me, too." Before he could find a good reason not to, his arms encircled her waist. With her body flush to his, more than his heart grew warm. "It's been too long."

"Agreed." She smiled up at him.

He pressed his forehead to hers and released a slow breath.

They both stood rooted, for a long moment, breathing each other in.

Then she turned and took another step forward as the line moved. Her hand reached back and found his.

He twined their fingers and hauled her against him. Her sweet round bottom in a perfectly fitted pair of jeans pressed against him. His control faltered.

He breathed in. The scent of her shampoo, coconut and pineapple, filled his senses.

The line moved another couple of steps forward.

Luke didn't want to budge. He wanted to stay rooted to his spot, with Julie, and forget everything else. The past. The craziness. The now.

The couple in front of them moved. He and Julie were up next to order. She leaned into him a little more.

Too soon, the line cleared, and it was their turn. She stepped aside, moving elbow to elbow.

"The usual?" he asked.

She nodded, reaching inside her purse.

He frowned. "Two plates of brisket."

Glancing at her, he added, "And lunch is on me."

The attendant nodded. "Drinks?"

Luke confirmed.

The young guy stuck out two cups.

Julie took them as Luke paid.

Yeah. This felt a lot like old times. They were damn good times, too. He wasn't kidding when he'd said those months with her was the best time of his life. He'd just been too stubborn and too young to realize letting her go would almost kill him.

"What do you want to drink?"

"Surprise me."

Luke piled mashed potatoes and beans on their plates as she manned the drinks stand. They got their usual booth in the corner.

And for a second, life didn't feel as if it was tilted, slowly spinning off its axis.

The moment wouldn't last.

This case would be over as soon as Luke found Rob. And he would find the SOB. Julie would return to her normal life. To Herb. And Luke would settle into his routine again.

Even though letting her go had almost killed him, he'd survived, hadn't he?

Because suddenly, the thought of trying to live without Julie was a sucker punch and he couldn't breathe.

*Shake it off.*

He slid onto the wooden bench across from her.

Every bit of him wanted to move across the table and snuggle in beside her, but he needed to keep his head clear.

A few bites into his meal, his cell buzzed. He fished it out of his pocket. The name on the screen read Bill Hightower.

What was the local newscaster doing calling Luke?

"Campbell here."

"Sir, this is—"

"I know who this is. Can you advise me of the nature of the call?"

"Something showed up in a studio here at the TV station that I think you'll be interested in seeing."

"Mind giving me a hint?"

"It's a message. A note for you. From a guy who calls himself Ravishing Rob."

"Did you touch it?"

"I'm afraid so. No one knew what we had at first."

The original prints might've been damaged. Luke bit back a curse. "Who discovered it?"

"One of my producers." The normally even-toned newscaster sounded a little rattled.

"Keep it somewhere safe. Don't touch it. I'll be there in ten minutes." Luke motioned for Julie to finish eating as he ended the call.

"Who was that?"

"A TV reporter. Said he has a message from Rob."

"That where we're headed?" She'd already grabbed her purse and was sliding out of the booth.

"I need to take a look at the evidence. I want to know where Rob left it. Check the area. Talk to the staff. Maybe someone saw something. We'll head to Austin afterward if we can't get an address on Camden. Since we're getting a late start, we'll plan to stay over." The thought of spending the night with Julie in a hotel room didn't do good things to Luke's libido.

"Okay."

"Obviously, my place has been compromised."

"Understood."

On their way out, Luke phoned his boss about Rick and

updated him on the gray late-model sedan, too. His next call was to his older brother, Nick, but he didn't pick up.

On the walk to his truck, Julie slipped her hand in his. Friends? Could he limit their relationship? She felt a lot like home.

The drive downtown to the TV station took longer than he'd expected. Traffic was heavy, which doubled his time.

There was no close parking, so Luke parked in a nearby garage and opened the door for Julie. She made no move to hold his hand again. His mind was elsewhere, and she seemed to understand why.

Even though he'd stopped talking, he hoped she understood this was different. He was still available. This was focus, not completely shutting her out.

Their silence was warm and companionable as they walked the street filled with luxury hotels and apartments. This urban area was like so many, one block upscale, the next graffiti-covered walls and empty beer cans lined the streets.

Workers huddled near doors, smoking.

An argument broke out a few feet in front of them between two men in suits. Fists flew and the crowd parted, creating a circle around the action.

Luke shot Julie a look before jogging toward the pair. "Break it up. I'm Special Agent Campbell, and I don't want to have to arrest either of you."

He tapped the badge on his waistband.

The younger man took a step back and touched his lip. Drops of blood trickled down his chin. "He busted my lip. He wasn't supposed to do that."

He made a move toward the other guy. Luke stepped in between them, his palm flat against Young Guy's chest.

"What do you mean he wasn't *supposed* to do that?"

"Some dude paid us three hundred dollars each to pretend like we were fighting."

A diversion? Luke glanced toward where he'd left Julie. She was gone.

A loud scream split the air.

"Julie." Damn that he'd allowed himself a moment of distraction. She might pay for his mistake with her life. The feeling of guilt and shame washed over him as his body trembled. The all-too-familiar feelings rushed him.

Luke pushed through the crowd toward the sound of the scream. Where was Julie?

He bolted through the bodies surrounding him. There was no sign of her.

His brain couldn't wrap around the fact Rob had her. Thinking about what he would do with her sent an icy chill down Luke's spine.

They couldn't have gotten far.

Worst-case scenarios drilled Luke's thoughts as he searched the street, running. Rob could have stuffed her into a waiting car.

The air thinned around Luke.

In that case, the bastard could already be on the highway heading almost anywhere. Luke cursed. If that was true, it could be game over.

Luke rounded the corner and stopped the first person he saw. "Did you see a woman with black hair come this way with a man?"

The person shook their head. "Sorry."

Anger coursed through Luke. This could not be happening. Period. He'd kept Julie next to him for a reason. Helplessness rolled through him in waves. He refused to acknowledge it. Instead, he rushed to the next person, who was on her cell, and asked the same question while flashing his badge.

She nodded and pointed south. "I'm on hold with the police. I saw a man dragging a woman that way. Couldn't get a good look at her. She was struggling."

"Stay on the phone with the police. Tell them everything you just told me," Luke instructed her as he bolted south, maintaining eye contact to ensure the woman understood.

"Okay. I will." Her voice rose from adrenaline.

"Tell them Special Agent Campbell needs backup." Luke broke into a dead run. His tremors returned. He couldn't even consider the possibility of not finding Julie. *Another few minutes, Rob gets her to a secure location, and it's over.*

Luke stopped at the intersection, glancing left then right. Nothing. She couldn't be gone.

This case was bringing back more of the past than his relationship with his ex.

A HAND COVERED Julie's mouth. She tried to bite it. Couldn't. He must've anticipated the move.

She jabbed her elbow back, connecting with his rib cage.

Her attacker swore. He dropped his hand to force her arms behind her back.

She finally broke free enough to scream again, praying Luke would be able to track her location. Had Rob dragged her too far? Had Luke realized she was gone yet?

Luke was good at his job. He would come, she reassured herself.

The next thing she knew, a bag or some kind of cloth material covered her head, and she was being dragged again. She kicked, wriggled and struggled against the vise-like grip around her hands—hands that had been shoved behind her back.

She managed another scream before she was dropped

and concrete slammed into her. Her head cracked against the unforgiving sidewalk.

He swore again, and then he was gone.

With her hands freed, she pulled off the covering in time to see Luke coming at a full run toward her. She pushed up to a sitting position as he stopped in front of her and dropped to his knees.

The haunted look on his face sent chills up her back.

"You all right?" He scanned the area.

"I'm fine. Go."

He took off in the direction she'd heard footsteps, hesitated, then circled back. "Might be playing into his hands by chasing him. He caught us off guard. I won't let it happen twice."

A small crowd had gathered around her.

Julie stood and shook off the shock. "Someone had to have seen him." She looked around. "Did any of you see what happened to me?"

A Hispanic male wearing a uniform stepped forward. "I was watching the fight. Then I heard a scream and turned to look over here, but by that time all I saw was the back of a man. He was taller than me. About this big." He held his hand up to indicate close to Luke's height.

"Around six feet?"

A few heads nodded in the crowd.

"Yeah. That seems about right. He looked like he might be a runner. Slim but athletic. A few inches shorter than you, maybe." He shrugged. "I couldn't see much more than that."

Luke thanked him, very aware of the fact that the height given matched that of the uniformed officer who'd shown up at Julie's place. "Did anyone else see the guy?"

Shoulders shrugged. A woman confirmed, "I think

that's a pretty good description. His back was turned, so I didn't get a look at his face."

After thanking the group, Luke turned to Julie. "I need to talk to the people who distracted us."

They jogged back to the spot of the earlier altercation. A pair of officers were interviewing the men who'd been involved in the fake fight.

Luke introduced himself, then turned to the older guy in a suit. "Tell me about the person who paid you."

"He was wearing a hoodie and sunglasses, but I could see that he had dark hair."

The young guy nodded in agreement.

"And you didn't think anything was wrong with the picture when he offered you money to fight?" Luke shot a heated look at them.

"Sure I did. At first. I said no," the young guy piped up.

"What changed your mind?"

"He seemed like a nice guy. Said he was playing a prank on his roommate. That it was his birthday. We weren't actually supposed to throw punches." He sneered at the older guy.

"And you believed him?"

"Honestly, I thought I was on one of those TV prank shows at first. Then I thought, what could it hurt?" The young guy shrugged. Looking toward the uniformed officer, he asked, "Am I under arrest?"

The officer shot a glance toward Luke.

"No," Luke said. "But give your information to this officer for his report. If we need to talk to you again, we'll be in touch." He hesitated. "And the next time someone asks you for a favor, I'd suggest you both walk away."

"You bet I will," the young man said.

Luke clamped his hand around Julie's, gripping her tightly. "Let's check in at the TV station."

Another block and they stood in front of American Airlines Stadium. Luke located the glass doors at the entrance to the station and guided them toward the door. Julie's body still shook from adrenaline and fear, and she noticed a tremble in Luke's hand, too.

The big and brave Luke had never seemed quite so vulnerable to her before. Even when he came back from the war, he seemed more angry than anything else. Afraid? No.

He stopped at the door and turned to her. "You okay?"

"Yeah. I'd be lying if I didn't admit to being shaken up, but I'm fine."

"That's my girl." He pressed a kiss to her forehead. "I can drop you off at the police station if you want out. You'd be safe there." His gaze bored deeply into hers. His brown eyes filled with worry and what looked a lot like fear.

"As long as I'm with you, I'll be all right," she reassured him.

"But he got…to…you." His voice broke on the last word.

"And you saved me, Luke."

He took in a sharp breath. "Not good enough. You're sure you want to go through with this? I can take you back to the ranch. There's enough law enforcement crawling in and out of there on a daily basis to ensure your safety. I know Gran would like to see you again."

"Me, too. As soon as all this is cleared, I'd like to go out for a visit. I miss her." The warmth in his gaze nearly knocked her back a step.

This time he planted a kiss on her lips before leading her into the news studio.

The receptionist was a cute and perky brunette. She asked them to wait while she paged the newscaster. An armed guard stood sentinel behind her, nodding toward Luke.

Julie immediately recognized Bill Hightower the second he stepped into the lobby. He was shorter in person than he looked on TV. Blond hair, blue eyes and a million-dollar smile with perfectly straight white teeth. He looked to be in his mid- to late-thirties. He had a crisp, new-car-salesman look about him. Suit on, he was polished and ready for the camera.

His hand jutted out in front of Luke, who accepted the shake without a lot of enthusiasm. For whatever reason, Luke didn't seem to care much for this person.

"I wish you were here under different circumstances." Bill's lips curled down in a frown. His brow furrowed.

Julie had to give it to him—he could sell his words. Maybe a bit too perfectly?

"As do we," Luke said, not appearing affected or impressed by the newscaster's plastic concern.

"It's a pleasure to meet you, Special Agent Campbell. You already know I've been wanting an interview with you for months. I understand you're here for a different reason, but while I have you, I wonder if you'd consider answering a few questions?"

"Call me Luke." He paused. The muscle in his jaw ticked. "You said on the phone that you have something for me."

"Yes. I do," he stalled.

"Then, if you don't mind, I'd like to see it."

The reporter turned his attention toward Julie and put on a charming smile. "And you are?"

"Julie Davis."

Luke stepped in between them, drawing the reporter's blue-eyed gaze. "If we could see the message, we'll get out of your way. I'm sure you're busy and I'd hate to be underfoot."

"No trouble at all."

"Is it here at the front?" Luke pressed.

"No. Follow me." Bill led them down the hall to his office, stopping at the door. He motioned toward a pair of leather chairs as he perched on his desk. "Any chance this is actually from the serial killer you've been following?"

"You know I can't comment on an ongoing investigation." Luke parted his feet in an athletic stance and folded his arms. He'd be intimidating to most men, standing at his full six-foot-one height.

Bill seemed to dismiss the threat. "Then it *is* part of the investigation?"

"I haven't seen the message yet." Luke cracked a smile meant to ease the tension.

"Would you both mind holding on for a minute?"

Luke said he didn't, but his expression told another story. Julie knew him inside and out. She doubted the reporter picked up on Luke's frustration. She could see that he was growing increasingly annoyed.

The reporter disappeared, returning a few moments later with a tentative smile. Was he nervous?

Julie certainly understood the newscaster's trepidation. Rob was a monster. And a desperate one at that. Or was there something else going on?

A shiver raced up her spine thinking about how close she'd just come to being dragged to some random place in that psycho's clutches. Trapped. Icy fingers closed around her heart and squeezed at the memory.

She blew out a breath. Her quick thinking had most likely saved her life. Fighting had worked. No matter what else Rob tried to do, she wouldn't be an easy target. Julie planned to fight.

She already knew what would happen if he got her to another location. He'd been so close moments before. Just thinking about it made her skin sting like a thousand fire-ant bites. She shivered, remembering that the best way to escape a sicko was not to let him take you to a second site. Thank God Luke arrived when he had. She couldn't remember where, but she'd read that an abductor all but assured no possibility of escape if he could get his victim to a different spot where it would be harder to break free.

If she'd had to force the man to snap her neck on the street corner, she would not give him the satisfaction of performing his ritual murder on her.

She was not one of his *projects*.

Bill returned, easing onto his desk, and used a nail clipper to pick up a piece of paper and a hair ribbon.

If the items had been there all along, why did Bill disappear down the hall pretending to go get them?

"It's probably too late, but I secured these from Hair and Makeup on the off chance his print is still there."

Wasn't he being helpful?

Luke eyed the reporter suspiciously, took a small paper bag from his back pocket and nodded. "Much appreciated."

He examined the paper. Deep frown lines bracketed his mouth.

Julie moved closer to get a look.

On the handwritten note was printed "I could be anywhere. Even here. The Devil's in the details, but rest assured, the body count is about to rise."

## Chapter Eight

Another cold chill trickled down Julie's spine as she glanced around. He could be anywhere. Even there. Watching.

Bill clasped his hands and leaned forward. "The note isn't signed. Is this actually a message from Ravishing Rob?"

"No comment." Luke's tone was cold. His temper was on a short leash.

"So you're not denying it?" the reporter pressed.

"No comment." Luke closed the paper bag. "Where did you find this?

"I didn't."

Luke ate the real estate between them with a couple of quick strides. His hand fisted when he stood over the man who cowered on his desk. "Look. You want to play games with me? Is that your best move right now, Mr. Hightower? You want to spend the night in jail for obstructing an on-going investigation?"

"No."

A soft knock at the door turned them around. A small woman stood behind them, holding a white piece of paper with a scribble on it.

Bill motioned for her to come in. After handing him the note, she immediately excused herself and disappeared down the hall without making eye contact with Julie or Luke. That couldn't be a good sign.

"One of my producers discovered them taped to a camera lens." Bill sounded distracted. Whatever she'd handed him got his full attention.

"Which one?" Luke took a step back.

"In the studio."

"I thought the newsroom was secure."

"It's supposed to be."

"How'd the note get there?"

"No one saw anyone come in." Bill shrugged. "I have a few questions for you. Unless you plan to get in my face again."

"You didn't answer mine."

"Funny. You didn't respond to my request for an interview last month. Or the one before that. Or the one before that. Can you give us any idea of Rob's profile? People deserve to know. Otherwise, you're allowing a killer to walk around invisible."

"I'd like to speak to the person who found the note."

Bill didn't make a move. "There are no killers here. I have no reason to believe the person who left this note is an employee of the station."

"That's not your call to make." The pieces fit together. Someone had left the note knowing the person who found it would call the agent in charge of the investigation, who happened to have the killer's new target in protective custody.

The newscaster didn't budge.

"You don't want to talk here? We can head to Lew Sterrett Justice Center if you think everyone would be more comfortable having a conversation there." Luke's steel gaze centered on Bill.

"Fine. The guy who found the note is a producer on the

morning show. His name is Lowell Duncan." Bill loosened his tie, then pushed a buzzer on the phone and asked to see Duncan.

Not five minutes later, a sloppily dressed man in his mid-forties stood at the door. Didn't fit the description of the killer Luke had described, but then, he'd also said it could be almost anyone.

One glance toward Luke told her he was sizing this guy up.

"Come in, Lowell," Bill said sharply.

It was clear the two didn't have a warm-and-fuzzy relationship.

"Sir."

Bill gestured toward Luke. "Special Agent Campbell would like a word with you."

Lowell turned. "Yes, sir. I'm guessing this is about the note I found."

"It is. I appreciate your time. You must be busy keeping this place in line." Luke extended his hand to Lowell. The man smiled and took the hand being offered.

Lowell's tense expression softened as he nodded.

"Can you show me where you found the note?"

"Sure." Lowell turned and backtracked down the hall toward the studio.

Julie stayed close to Luke as they walked down the hall. The room where the morning show was taped was smaller than she'd anticipated. Three walls of windows didn't afford a lot of privacy, either.

Lowell stopped at the threshold. "There's a live broadcast going. But I can point to the camera."

He motioned toward the one positioned front and center, aimed toward the newscaster. "It was here when I came on this morning at four o'clock to work *Good Morning Sun.*"

Lowell shoved his hands in his pockets and balanced on the balls of his feet.

"Which entrance do you use to get to work?"

"The one in the alley."

"Did you see anyone around this morning on your way in to work? Anyone hanging around back there?"

"No. Nothing out of the ordinary."

"What about inside the studio? Was anything else unusual delivered or did you see anyone who didn't belong?"

"Nothing out of place. I checked everything. It's part of my morning ritual. The fools on my crew like to mess with me. I never know what's going to happen when I unscrew a lid anymore." He held his hands up, palms out.

"But you didn't call it in until much later? What made you hold on to it?"

"I'm sorry about that. Thought it was a trick at first."

Luke nodded his understanding. Julie figured growing up with a couple of brothers, he could relate.

"What made you decide to call it in?"

"No one claimed responsibility by the end of the show." He glanced from Luke to Julie and seemed to realize neither of them knew when that was. "It's over at ten o'clock."

Luke glanced at his watch. "Does someone always come forward by now? When they play a practical joke?"

Lowell half smiled. "Seems to be half the fun for these buffoons. Getting away with it is the first kick. Laughing about it when it's over comes in a close second. None of the guys even knew it was there."

"How many work on the show?"

"Three full-timers. I've got one intern."

"Are they here by any chance?"

"Nah. They left a few hours ago after the wrap."

Luke cocked an eyebrow.

"I have them come in my office and we talk about what

worked, what didn't. See what we can improve for next time." Lowell had a genuine quality to him. Julie figured he'd make a good boss. Heck, a good person. She wasn't so sure about Bill Hightower.

"I'll need to follow up with them," Luke said. "Can I have a list of names?"

"Sure." Lowell rubbed the scrub on his chin. You need me to round them up? I can call them in if you'd like."

"No. Thank you. I'll swing by in the morning."

"I'll put your name on the list. Feel free to watch the show."

"Will do." Luke smiled. His laid-back expression told Julie he believed Lowell. "Do you always come in at four?"

"Usually. Not much traffic to contend with at that hour, so I'm generally right on time. Maybe a little early some days."

"And you're sure there was nothing different about this morning?"

"Nope. No, sir." He paused as if to take a moment to check his thoughts. "I started to rip it up and toss it in the can, but then Mr. Hightower showed up. I told him what had happened, and he asked to see the note."

"He gets here around ten to do the lunch news?"

"Has to. It's in his contract." Lowell froze as if he'd said something wrong. "I'm sure he would anyway."

Luke nodded. "Then what happened?"

"Next thing I know, I'm being asked to talk to you."

"I appreciate your time, Lowell. Is there an easy way to reach you if I have more questions?"

"I'm almost always here at the station. My house is a few blocks away. I can give you my cell. But the receptionist keeps me on a short leash." He chuckled. "The station always knows where to find me."

Bill reappeared as Luke made a move toward the lobby.

Bill's gaze trained on Julie. "Tell me, Agent Campbell, is it ethical for you to work on a case involving your ex-wife?"

The two men locked eyes.

Luke's eyes flashed fire. "Thank you for your time."

Bill must've realized his story was about to walk out the door. He stood in between them and the exit. "I can keep a secret if it's for a good reason."

"You sure you want to do that?" Luke turned to the reporter and took a menacing step forward, poking his finger in Bill's chest. "Threaten me?"

"I—uh—"

"That really your best move?"

"No, sir."

"Good. I'll be back and I expect your full cooperation. Understood?"

Bill nodded slowly.

Luke twined his and Julie's fingers and stalked toward the exit.

The reporter stayed rooted to his spot. Smart move.

"That guy was a jerk. What the heck's going on with him?" she asked when they were out in the fresh air again.

"Maybe he's just a jerk wanting an exclusive." Luke held tight to her hand.

"Where to next? Austin?"

Luke already had his phone out of his pocket. He let go of her hand long enough to make a call. His first was to Detective Garcia to update him on all that had happened. The next was to his boss. He finished the call as they located the truck. "No. That trip's on hold for the time being. We need to drop off the evidence at the lab before we do anything else. They grab a print and there's no road trip necessary. We'll find our guy."

"How about after that?"

"I realized we have one more location in Addison. One

in Dallas. Then we'll think about hitting the road. The team should be able to lift prints quickly if there's anything to work with on that piece of paper. And we know Rob's here."

Luke started the engine and snaked out of the parking garage, glancing in his rearview mirror.

"What is it?"

"Either someone at the station is involved, or Rob planted the note to make sure we went there." The anger in his tone nearly took her breath away.

"So he could get us out in public? It's not like we're hiding. We've been in plain sight all day."

"True, but he didn't know where we were before. And he ambushed us. He might have been trying to flush us out all along by bringing us to the station. He could've been there hiding since this morning." Luke's jaw ticked. "Or it's possible Hightower faked the note."

"Why would he do that?"

"He's been after me for an interview for months. He could've set up the scenario in an attempt to get me to the station. And our guy could've been following us, waiting for a chance to snatch you."

"A reporter wouldn't resort to this, would he? Isn't that a crime?" Was that why Luke had such a bitter response to Bill Hightower? Or had he just had bad experiences with reporters in general? There was something about their interaction that had Julie wondering what else was between the two of them.

And those last words, the ones about her and Luke. Could Hightower cause problems for Luke at work?

"He did an investigative report on the FBI and tried to dig into my past to expose me, questioning whether or not I could do my job. And, yes, it's a crime."

"I don't remember reading anything in the news about you. What a jerk. I'm so sorry someone would do that."

"He didn't succeed. My boss struck a deal with him so he wouldn't run his story. He kept it quiet in exchange for information."

"Your boss must think a lot of you to do that."

"We take care of our own."

"What he did doesn't seem ethical."

"Believe me, reporters have stepped over the line more than once to get a story. And this guy is no exception." Luke's cell buzzed. He glanced at the screen and then locked eyes with Julie.

"Or maybe this whole thing has been a wild-goose chase meant to distract us so Rob could kill again."

# Chapter Nine

"Oh. God. No. What happened?" Julie fought the panic closing her windpipe.

"We're heading north. The house of a twenty-seven-year-old woman is being broken into. A neighbor called in a suspicious-person report. The guy's wearing a hoodie and sunglasses." He hit the gas pedal and sped out of the parking structure.

Julie sat perfectly still, watching as Luke punched data into his laptop at every red light on the road heading north. He'd avoided taking the Tollway since there was a wreck reported, instead opting for a straight shot up Preston Road.

Driving to Plano took less than ten minutes.

Another few minutes that ticked by like years, and they pulled in front of a large two-story brick house. The lawns were neatly manicured in the suburb—a safe place with good schools where bad things weren't supposed to happen. Julie realized heinous crimes could occur anywhere. Recent events had taught her if someone fixated on her there wasn't much anyone could do to stop him. Even a skilled FBI agent like Luke could barely keep her safe.

"Keep close to me." The rich timbre in Luke's voice softened his command.

He parked in front of the residence and palmed his weapon, leading with his gun.

Luke approached the house cautiously. The front door was unlocked, so he turned the knob slowly and shot Julie a look. The overwhelming smell of bleach assaulted her as she stepped inside the door behind him.

Step by step, she followed him into the living area. A glance to the right nearly knocked Julie off her feet. She stumbled backward the moment her eyes made contact with the victim.

The woman's body had been neatly arranged on the couch. Some blood was splattered, but there was surprisingly little. Bleach had been poured on her clothing. But the severed head made Julie's stomach twist, nearly doubling her over. Bile burned the back of her throat, and she tasted vomit.

Luke tucked her behind him, cursing. His massive shoulder blocked most of her view.

The only thing holding her together was Luke. She heard him whisper an apology as he continued through the house, checking behind every door, in each room, every closet.

Sirens wailed in the distance, roaring toward them. Luke had notified local police he was inside the house.

Moments later, lights blared from the street. Luke palmed his badge and met the officers in the yard, tightening his grip on Julie's hand.

"The house is clear," he said to the nearest officer. He relayed other information as Julie stood there, stunned.

The officer thanked Luke and headed toward the front door.

Thinking about what was inside sent a wave of nausea rippling through Julie. "What does he do with the...head?"

"He takes special care with cleaning it," he said in a low voice. "Always puts it in a different place after he chops some hair off. Like a twisted game of hide-and-seek. It's his signature."

"He takes a piece of their hair? What does he do with it?" Julie could scarcely contain her horror.

The answer hit her fast and hard. "He's making a human wig, isn't he?"

Luke didn't answer. Didn't have to. Julie could see from his expression she was right. "This was him, then. I could tell she had black hair."

"Looks like it."

"When did he…?"

"Not long ago."

"How do you know?"

"Normally, we can tell by the blood. When the heart stops, it pools inside the body, so in her position, it was at her feet and ankles."

"You saw that?"

He nodded, his gaze intent on her.

"One look at her and I froze," Julie said. "The bleach. You mentioned that before." She wrinkled her nose involuntarily. "Why does he use it?"

"Makes forensic evidence harder to find, for one. Not impossible, but difficult. Even so, I think it goes deeper than that. He sees these women as unclean, which is how he justifies his actions."

"So, he's cleansing them?"

Luke nodded. "And then punishing them."

Julie trained her gaze on the ground, unable to keep the tears from her eyes or hold her composure. Her stomach revolted.

Before she realized what was happening, his hand was low on her back, ushering her toward the truck.

The chilly breeze was a welcome respite on her warm

cheeks. She stepped on the curb just in time for the first heave.

Luke held her hair off her face and whispered words of comfort.

Embarrassment edged in as her heaves became productive. "I'm sorry."

"Don't be."

Looking at him now, he was different but stronger. Could she continue to let him be her strength?

Even after all they'd been through?

When she really thought about it, she had a habit of being with men who shut themselves off emotionally.

Her father had never been there for her. Not even when her mother died. Julie had been a little girl. She remembered the day vividly. It was the first day of kindergarten. She knew her mother had been sick, but no one had prepared her for the fact her mom might die.

Coming home to the news had made her close herself off, too.

Especially when her father hugged her once, then told her they had to get tight and move on.

Most of her childhood memories had faded, but Julie knew exactly the last time she was hugged by both of her parents that first day of school. Julie hadn't understood the tears her mom shed that morning. She thought they had been for the fact she was going to school.

Little did she know her mom would be gone by the time she got home.

Julie hated first days.

From that day forward, she'd get sick in the pit of her stomach at all firsts. And especially when summer ended and school started again.

Her mother had been the soft, emotional one. Her father

had been all about self-discipline and order. Physically, he was always present, but emotionally? Butch Davis didn't do emotions.

Instead of tucking her into bed at night, he had morning inspections. By the second week of school, Julie had learned how to make her own bed and pass muster.

That first night, he took down all the pictures of her mother and neatly packed them away in boxes, storing them in the attic. He never went up there again. Not even when they moved two years later.

The worst part of the whole ordeal was that he never talked about her mother. Ever. It was as if she'd never existed to him. And Julie knew on instinct she wasn't supposed to talk about her mother, either. He'd remarried before the first anniversary of her death.

There were no complaints about her stepmother. She was a nice woman who cleaned when she got nervous. Supper was on time every day. Six o'clock. Very little real conversation was ever had at the dinner table or anywhere else, for that matter.

Was that why Julie was so lost when it came to talking about her own feelings? Why she couldn't for the life of her find the words to help Luke when he was drowning emotionally after Iraq?

Deep down inside, she knew her father had done the best he could. He'd dealt with what life had thrown at him the only way he knew how. She didn't hate him for her childhood. He'd provided all the basic necessities of a roof over her head and food in her stomach. His way of dealing with emotion had been to shut down and ignore it. He'd developed heart disease in his fifties and joined her mother the same year she'd met Luke.

And yet, the Luke she'd met was nothing like her father. Maybe that was the big draw at first?

No one understood her better than Luke. No one made her laugh like Luke. No one caused her body to soar like Luke.

Theirs was a bond so strong, Julie had thought it to be unbreakable. And that was why she'd trashed every one of her rules and married him a month after they'd met. This kind of connection came along once in a lifetime, she'd reasoned. What they had was real and no one could take it away, she'd told herself.

She'd made herself a promise a long time ago that if she should ever get married and have a family of her own, she'd hug them every day. They would know how very much they meant to her every minute. Because life had taught Julie at an early age those she loved could be taken away in an instant.

She had no plans to waste hers by leaving those she loved wondering about her feelings. This was the relationship she'd thought she had with Luke.

And hadn't she?

Then he'd shipped off. She hadn't recognized the man who came home to her.

Determination forced her to stay in the relationship even after he'd quit. She'd thought surely she could bring him back. Their love could move mountains.

"I know this is hard," he soothed, snapping her mind back to the present—a place she was no longer convinced she wanted to be.

Besides, sure Luke was there for her now, but how long before the wire tripped again and he went all emotional desert on her?

She'd been naive the first time she'd fallen for him. Lucky for her, experience was a good teacher.

"Dammit, Luke. I'm fine."

THE FACT SHE swore didn't mean good things. Luke also didn't like her sharp tone, because it signaled she was overwhelmed.

Of course she was. She wasn't the first person who'd had a visceral reaction to her first crime scene. Technically, it was her second, but she'd been in shock during the first, so it wasn't the same. Her mind was fully aware this time. Processing every sight, smell, sound. Taking everything in.

"We don't have to be here," he soothed.

"I don't want to get in the way of your case. You need to investigate. I can handle this."

"My team will be here to process the scene. The sergeant looks like he has everything under control until then. Nothing says we have to stay." He thumbed away a tear rolling down her cheek.

"I'm in the way."

"No. You're right where you need to be."

She looked up at him with those amber eyes—eyes filled with pain—and his heart squeezed. Another chink in his armor obliterated. Spending time together was a mistake. All his good memories came crashing down, suffocating him at the thought of walking away from her again.

If there was another place to stash her, somewhere far away from him, he would do it.

The reality? He was her best hope.

He'd already thought about sending her to Europe or Mexico to hide. Hell, he'd pay for the trip out of his own pocket if it would do any good.

Rob wanted Julie. He would go to the ends of the earth

to find her. He seemed to know where they were at every step. Had he gotten close enough to bug Luke's truck?

The guy had skills.

Too bad he was on the other side of the law. Luke could use someone with Rob's abilities, if not his morals, on his team.

Not happening. The guy was a cold-blooded killer. Another woman was dead because Luke couldn't get a step ahead of Rob.

Shame and guilt ate away at Luke's stomach lining.

"Luke."

"Yeah."

Those eyes pierced through him. "Get me out of here."

She'd seen enough for one day. He wanted to give her one night of peace.

By the time they reached his truck, his team had texted their location. They were a couple of blocks away. They'd be there in less than five minutes.

Luke checked for a device under his truck and then under the hood. He didn't find anything, which didn't mean much. Gadgets were so small these days they were virtually undetectable. He made a mental note and moved on.

He'd most likely cross paths with his team on the way out of the neighborhood because he needed to stay put for a minute and update the file.

Luke keyed in information before starting the truck and pulling away.

The signature on this killing was Rob's. But the timing was off. Why so soon? What did this murder have to do with Julie?

If Rob was trying to flush them out, he had. He'd been dictating their movements all day, Luke realized.

"Are you thirsty?"

"I could use some water," Julie said, staring out the front window. Her color was slowly returning.

Luke pulled into the first convenience store he could find.

"I need a bathroom, if that's okay," Julie said.

He led her to the back of the place and stood guard at the door.

Five minutes later, he knocked. "Everything okay in there?"

"I'm almost done. I'll be out in a minute."

Another couple of uncomfortable minutes and she came out. She'd pulled her hair back in a ponytail and, from the looks of it, had splashed water on her face.

"Better?"

"I had to get that taste out of my mouth. Luckily, I always keep a travel toothbrush and toothpaste in my purse."

Jealousy flashed through him with the speed of a lightning bolt. Why did she keep those items close at hand? Logic told him it was in case she slept over at her boyfriend's.

Luke walked to the drinks case and pulled two bottled waters.

He had no business knowing why she kept those items in her bag. Anything outside of this case was none of his business. So why did a voice in the back of his head say, *She's mine?*

Julie wasn't *his* anymore. No matter how much it felt like old times being near her. And not just any times, but the good times. He had a life apart from her. She had a boyfriend.

He let silence sit between them as he paid for their water. She followed him to the truck, where he opened her door for her.

Luke made a move to close the door but stopped.

A question was eating away at him.

Before he let this—whatever this was—go any further between the two of them, he had to know.

"Is it serious between you two?"

mistake twice. What was that old saying? *Fool me once,
shame on you. Fool me twice, shame on me.* Sure it was a
cliché, but it worked for her.

She closed her eyes and leaned her head against the
headrest. Images assaulted her. She rubbed her eyes and
then opened them.

Luke pulled into a parking garage, found a spot and
then cut the engine. "What is it, Julie?"

"This. My life. It's so screwed up that I can't begin to
sort through it." She wasn't just talking about Rob, but she
didn't want Luke to know. She wasn't ready to discuss their
relationship—a relationship that confused her as much as
comforted her. "Where are we?"

"Safe house." He hopped out and was at her side before
she could reach for the door handle. His lips were curved
in a frown. His disposition had shifted to dark and moody.

Was he still bothered by her admission? False or not,
she'd done her best to sell it.

The parking garage was active. Well-dressed couples
held hands, walking toward either the elevator or the stairs.

"Where are we?"

"There are condos above the shops on this street. This
garage will conceal my truck."

"It's busy here. Is it safe to get out?"

"We'll blend in." He placed his hand on the small of
her back and electricity shot through her. Unfair that his
touch could heat her body so easily.

They moved to the street and into the crowd of forty-
somethings as they made their way down the tree-lined
road. There were plenty of couples, but single people were
abundant, too. Small groups of women looked as if they
were out for girls' night. Pairs of men were on the hunt.
The place was bustling with restaurants and shops.

"What time is it?" Julie had barely noticed that it had

## Chapter Ten

"What?" The question caught her off guard. How did Julie tell Luke that his memory was enough to stop her from being able to get close to any other man?

Should she tell him?

What could she possibly accomplish by pouring her soul out to the one man who'd stomped on her heart? Not to mention the fact that if a serial killer hadn't brought Luke to her doorstep, they wouldn't be speaking right now. If he'd come on his own terms, she could trust his feelings. But this? No.

"We've known each other for a while."

"Oh."

She steeled herself against the pain in his voice. Her heart begged her to tell him the truth. Herb was barely in the picture right now. No man before or since Luke had broken through her walls. He was her kryptonite.

Was that such a good thing?

He'd walked out once without looking back. What would stop him from doing it again?

Neither one seemed to feel like talking on the road. Julie didn't. Not after what she'd seen. Then there were her mixed-up feelings for Luke to contend with. Being with him was the first time she'd felt home in years—ever. And yet, her mind couldn't wrap around making the same become dark outside. Her nerves were stretched thin from the day's events. Images from the crime scene would haunt her for the rest of her life. She wondered if she'd ever be able to close her eyes again without seeing those horrible crimes relived in her nightmares.

"Eight-thirty." He led her to an elevator, pushed the button and waited. "I'll pick up something for supper once we're settled."

She hadn't eaten since lunch, which had been interrupted. Seriously doubted she could now. "I'm not hungry."

"I know. But you need to get something in your stomach. There's a deli on the corner. They make a great panini and tomato soup." His words were crisp and held a sharp edge, which was probably a good thing. Was he still thinking about what she'd said? Good. Because one touch and he'd melt her resolve.

"I'll try."

The elevator doors opened, closed. They stopped on the fifth floor.

Julie followed Luke down the hallway, feeling the weight of the day in every step.

"I called ahead and had someone bring clothing. You want to jump into the shower while I get food?"

"No." How did she tell him? Admit her vulnerability? Should she come straight out with it? "I...I'm scared, Luke."

His arm encircled her waist as they walked down the hallway. "You know I'm not going to let anything happen to you, right."

It wasn't a question.

She nodded as his arm tightened around her, sending currents of electricity pulsing through her body.

He stopped in front of the door, leaned over and then

pressed a kiss into her hair. She leaned into him as he worked the key.

The first thing she noticed when she walked across the threshold was how beautiful and plush the apartment was. The feminine decor was tastefully done. This was clearly not a bachelor pad. She wasn't exactly sure why she thought it would be. "Who provides these places?"

"Nice, isn't it?"

"'Gorgeous' is more like it. Surely this doesn't belong to the government." One look at the hand-scraped hardwood floors and high-end appliances in the open-concept kitchen and she could tell this most certainly was not something Uncle Sam would provide. The sky was clear and she could see lights all the way from downtown Dallas.

"It serves a purpose. Make yourself comfortable." He went to the kitchen cabinet and pulled out two glasses, then retrieved a bottled water from the fridge. He seemed to know his way around rather well.

Had she even known him before he'd left for duty? She believed she had, but she'd been wrong about so much in their life together. She'd also been naive enough to think they could get through anything as long as they were together.

Look how that had turned out.

Julie leaned into the sofa, half listening to Luke call in their dinner order. She heard him end the call as the sound of his footsteps drew closer.

"One of the officers downstairs volunteered to pick up our food."

She smiled, trying to erase the horrible images from her mind. "You want to walk downstairs with me to get it?"

"No. I'll wait here."

"Then keep this with you." He placed a small handgun

on the coffee table. "You remember what I taught you about shooting?"

She remembered a lot of things. And that was most likely her biggest problem now. "Yes."

"Okay. The safety's on. There are officers stationed around the building. Don't answer the door for anyone. You can reach me on my cell. I won't be long." He walked right to her, planted a firm kiss on her lips and then locked the door behind him.

Julie hugged a throw pillow to her chest.

Her cell buzzed. She retrieved it from her purse. Luke had sent a text checking on her. She let him know she was fine and then turned on the gas fireplace.

Sleep would come about as easily as snow in a Texas summer, but fatigue was catching up with her, so she leaned back and closed her eyes.

The image of her client and the innocent woman from earlier had stamped her thoughts.

Sobs broke free before she could suppress them. Tears flooded her eyes.

The doorknob turned. She palmed the gun and held her breath until she saw Luke's face. His presence brought a sense of warmth and calm over her.

He locked the door, set the food on the coffee table and dropped to his knees in front of her. "You're shaking."

She folded into his arms.

Before she could stop herself, her fingers mapped the strong muscles in his back. His hands were on her, then circled around her head, pulling her toward home.

He kissed her with a tenderness that caused a flutter in her stomach.

She wanted to erase the images from her mind, lose herself in the moment and forget about real life where people were hurt and Luke had been with other women.

He deepened the kiss and all rational thought flew out of her mind. One word overtook all others. "More."

JULIE ROSE FROM the sofa onto bent knees. She gripped the hemline of her shirt and pulled it over her head in one motion. All Luke could see was the flesh-colored lacy bra covering her full pert breasts.

"You're even sexier than I remember." He made a move to get up, to reduce the space between them.

Her hands gripped his shoulders before pushing him down. "You, stay right there."

Surrender never felt this much like heaven.

Her jeans hit the floor next and, glory of all glories, Luke's eyes feasted on the matching silk panties. He was already hard, and she seemed prepared to make this end before it began with the way her fingers lingered on the strap of her bra.

"Luke?"

"Yeah."

"I have to ask you a serious question before anything… before *this* can happen."

"You can have whatever you want." He held out his arms. "Take it."

She pushed him down to the floor and straddled him. "All kidding aside."

His body craved to be inside her so badly, he shook. He hoped like hell she was about to ask for more than one night. He'd promised himself a thousand times if he was ever lucky enough to get her back in his bed, he had no intention of letting her out.

"What is it?"

"Do you want me?"

"That's not a serious question."

Her amber eyes bored into him.

"Luke."

"Yeah."

"Do you want me?"

"What kind of question is that? Of course I want you. Do you see what you're doing to me?" He glanced down at his painfully stiff erection.

"I mean, *really* want me." She grabbed his wrists and pulled them above his head.

He looked into her eyes—eyes that possessed kindness, compassion and fire—everything he wanted in a woman. "More than I can ever say. More than you'll ever know. More than I'll ever deserve."

He broke free from her grasp. "I think it's pretty obvious I want this." He picked her up and took her to the bedroom, placing her on top of the duvet. He let his fingertip graze the vee between her breasts. "And this." His finger trailed down her belly to the waistline of her silk panties.

Her stomach quivered and a soft gasp drew from her lips.

He let his eyes take her in for a long moment before trailing his finger across her belly to her hip, making a line up her side. "And this."

"I missed how you fit me physically in every possible way. You have no idea how badly I want to wedge myself in between your thighs and thrust my way home again."

She started to speak but her words caught.

"But you know what?"

Her long dark lashes screened her eyes, but her face was flush with arousal. She shook her head.

"I miss this most of all." He pressed his finger to her forehead. "I miss the way you think. Your wit. How you know exactly what to say to make me laugh when I should be serious."

She restraddled him and then leaned down far enough to press her lips to his.

"I miss those, too."

She slowly pushed up to her knees, her gaze locked onto his the entire time.

Her body was grace and poetry in motion, and Luke couldn't help but stop to appreciate her movements. Yeah, she was sexy as all get-out, but she was so much more. He struggled for the words, the context, but sex with her was like rising to a whole new plane.

No one left him with the same feeling after as Julie had. Everyone else had met a physical need, and that was it.

He'd never known to expect more from a physical act.

She unhitched the silk bra she wore and tossed it to the side in one sweeping motion, releasing her ample breasts and pink nipples.

"You're beautiful." Luke made a move to touch her again, but she shoved him back down.

"Not yet."

"Keep this up and this'll be over before it begins," he half joked. Sex wasn't something he'd indulged in for a long time. The couple of women he'd been with after Julie had left him feeling hollow afterward. He figured he needed more time.

"I happen to know you have incredible stamina, Campbell." Her low, sexy voice rolled over him.

He pressed his palm on her belly. "Confession."

She looked at him.

"It's been a long time."

Her gaze widened.

"Surprised?"

"A guy like you could have pretty much anyone he wanted. I just figured—"

"Wrong. You figured wrong," he parroted, stroking her hip. "I didn't want anyone else."

The thought of someone else touching her could eat away his stomach lining, which was totally unfair. He wouldn't ask if she'd been with another man, with Herb.

She stared at him for a long moment. Her forehead wrinkled in that adorable way when she concentrated. "Confession."

The last thing he could stand hearing about would be her and another man. But he owed it to her to listen. After all, she never would've been with anyone else if he hadn't been such a jerk before. "You can tell me anything."

"I haven't been with anyone. Not since you."

"No one?" he repeated. His heart nearly burst out of his chest, filling with something that felt a lot like love. "Then it's been too long."

He tugged her down and wheeled her around, her breasts flush with his chest. He wasn't sure who managed to get her silk panties off, him or her, but he felt her sweet heat against his erection. Their hands and arms were a tangle, as were their legs as he moved in between the vee of her legs.

She arched her back as he drew figure eights on her sweet heat.

Her hand gripped his swollen erection.

Skin that was softer than silk pressed against him as she guided him inside her moist heat. One thrust and he was in deep. *Home.*

One hand continued working her mound and his other palmed her breast, all while he spread kisses along the nape of her neck. Sucking. Biting.

A low, sexy moan escaped as he rolled her nipple in

between his fingers, moving from one to the other, tugging and pulling as she moved her hips in rhythm with his.

Luke nearly exploded when he sensed her climax was near.

She moaned and rocked and whispered his name until he felt her muscles contracting around his length, and then he felt her burst into a thousand flecks of light.

Her rhythm didn't change as she coaxed him toward the same blissful release.

He thrust deeper and deeper as she flowered to take him in.

He groaned, low and feral, as complete rapture neared, every sense heightened.

Her sweet heat ground on his sex as he gripped her hips with both hands and pushed deeper until he detonated. Explosions rocked through him in the release only Julie could give him. His body tingled and pulsed afterward.

Heaving, he rolled over onto his back.

She turned to face him and settled into the crook of his arm.

He looked deep into her eyes and found everything he'd been missing for the past few years. And yet, now was not the right time for a distraction.

They'd taken the relationship well past friendship and he couldn't remember the last time he'd been this happy, but keeping her safe had to be his priority. "I didn't think I'd get this chance again. To be with you like this." He wanted to tell her he loved her, but he wasn't sure she was ready to hear the words any more than he could promise everything would work out differently this time. He didn't want to scare her away. Everything inside him said she felt the same way. He didn't need to hear the words. Yet. "I'm happy."

She blinked up at him, and he realized he was holding his breath.

The smile she gave him would have kept them warm through a blizzard. "Me, too."

All Luke's internal warning bells sounded. He was in deep with no way out. Hurting her again would kill him. But could he give her everything she deserved?

## Chapter Eleven

Julie nuzzled into Luke's side, where she reminded herself not to get too comfortable. Everything could change in an instant. Not that she needed the fact brought to her attention, especially with Rob a step ahead of them. Even a strong, capable man like Luke might not be able to keep the determined killer away.

"What are you thinking?" Luke kissed her forehead.

"About how much I missed this," she lied.

"Your eye twitched. You never were a good liar."

"This is nice. Us talking like this. I missed this."

"Me, too. You have no idea how much." His voice was low and had a gravel-like quality. He moved to face her, hauling her body flush with his and smiling a dry crack of a smile—his trademark. Those sharp brown eyes were all glittery with need. "You know what else would be 'nice'?" He pressed his erection to the inside of her thigh, sending heat to her feminine parts. His breath warmed her neck as he moved to her ear and whispered, "I can't get enough of you."

They made love slowly this time, savoring every inch of each other, as if both knew their time together could end in a flash.

A very real threat stalked her, determined as a pit bull.

And she'd learned the hard way there were no guarantees when it came to her and Luke.

He kissed her again before mumbling something about food. He disappeared down the hall, returning a minute later with plates balanced on his arms.

As they ate, he paused long enough to pepper kisses on her forehead, her nose, her chin. She surprised herself by getting a solid meal inside her.

Afterward, she fell into a deep sleep with her arms and legs entwined with Luke's.

The next morning, Julie blinked her eyes open.

She'd slept a solid eight. The bed was cold in the space Luke had occupied. She glanced around the room. His jeans were gone, but his shirt was crumpled on the floor.

Julie laid her head back on the pillow. The thought of her and Luke back together brought warmth and light into her heart. Would it last?

Clanking noises in the kitchen confirmed his presence in the apartment.

"Luke?"

"Be there in a minute. Don't move." He strolled in a moment later wearing jeans and a serious expression, holding two cups of coffee.

"Everything all right?"

"Yeah. Fine."

But was it? Something was on his mind. He was holding back. If they were going to think about having a relationship, this wouldn't cut it. She needed coffee to clear her head first. Then she had every intention of confronting Luke. She sat up and took the hot brew. *Heaven.*

Luke's cell buzzed before she could properly thank him.

He fished it from his pocket. "What's up?"

He said a few uh-huhs into the receiver before setting the phone down.

"What was that all about?"

"First things first." He leaned forward and pressed a kiss to her lips.

His breath smelled like a mix of peppermint toothpaste and coffee. Her new favorite combination. "What's going on?"

"My boss wants me to check out the news." He pulled a remote control from the bedside table and clicked on the thirty-two-inch flat-screen mounted on the wall.

Julie ignored the obvious reason he'd known it was there. He'd taken others here, maybe even women. A stab of jealousy pierced low in her belly. She refocused as Bill Hightower's face covered the screen. Below him was a ticker tape that read *Serial killer strikes again. Has the FBI been compromised?*

Hightower went on to talk about Luke guarding his ex-wife at the cost of taxpayers.

Luke picked up the phone and held it to his ear. He clenched his back teeth as he listened.

"I'm not leaving the case," he finally said.

He was silent for another long moment as though hearing out an argument.

"I know what he said, but I'm not handing her off to someone else." More beats of silence. "What would you do if this was your wife?"

The sound of the last word as it rolled off Luke's tongue sent tingles through her. She scooted closer to him and rested her cheek on his strong back.

"Take me off the case and you might as well kick me out of the Bureau. By giving away my relationship with Julie, he just made killing her more of a game for Rob."

Had Luke seen this possibility coming?

"I understand. Do what you need to do." He ended the call.

"Everything okay?" she asked as she took another sip of coffee.

"Yeah."

"Sounded like you got in trouble with your boss."

"No. He said what he needed to say."

"Is he taking you off the case?"

"No. It's fine. He trusts me."

"Luke, you're not telling me something." She sat up and faced the opposite wall.

He pulled her closer to him again without managing to spill a drop of her coffee. "That's better."

She couldn't argue being close to Luke was nice.

The look he gave her nearly stopped her heart. His gaze intensified. "Last night changed things between us, right?"

She nodded. "It did for me."

"Good."

Julie needed more time to process exactly how much things had changed, but this was a start. Could she trust it? Her logical mind said no even as her heart begged to disagree. "Maybe we got married too soon back then."

The hurt in his brown eyes nearly knocked her back. "It wasn't too soon for me. Was it for you?"

She didn't immediately answer.

"Do you regret marrying me?" His gaze didn't waver.

"No. It's not that. I was just thinking if we'd met now instead of then, maybe things would be different."

"I regret a whole lot of things. None of them have anything to do with the time I spent with you, Julie. You were the only thing I thought about when they captured me. Thinking about you kept me going no matter how hard they beat me or what else they did."

Pain serrated her heart at thinking about what he'd been forced to endure. No wonder all he wanted to do was close up and forget everything that had happened when he'd finally made it back home. "I'm sorry, Luke. I had no idea."

"How could you when I shut you out?"

"I just wish I could've been more comfort. If I'd known, maybe there was something I could've done to ease the pain."

He kissed her. Hard, then sweet. "I was an idiot. I blamed myself for everything that happened overseas. The shrink said I had signs of PTSD. I thought if you knew how weak I was, you'd leave me."

"Luke, I would never—"

"I know that now. It was in my head then. You didn't walk away. Not even when I pushed you."

Those beautiful brown eyes of his caused her stomach to free-fall. "Then why'd you force me to?"

"Every time you looked at me with pity in your eyes, I felt like less of a man. I came back broken…." Speaking the words looked as though they might kill him. His voice had gone rough. "No one could've convinced me I was worthy of being with you—you were sunshine and happiness and all those things I didn't know how to get back to. If I allowed myself to be happy, it seemed totally unfair to the men I lost."

"But it wasn't your fault. None of what happened to you was. Or them." She kissed him.

"They beat me, starved me, and that was okay. I was trained to handle physical abuse. It was nothing. Men died because of my decision." His voice cracked. "Jared was the baby. I was supposed to bring him home safe. What did I do? Got him killed."

"You wouldn't have done that on purpose."

"It was my fault we were in the situation in the first place. I take that to my grave. We were sent into a red zone. Command couldn't give us much detail about what we were walking into. By their best estimates, we had a little time before the enemy arrived." He paused, taking a deep breath. "We were in formation. Ready. Everything was cool. Then I saw something to my right I couldn't ignore. The area was supposed to be civilian free, but there was this little kid heading straight into the line of fire. I knew it was about to be a bloodbath. I'd killed plenty of men by then. But I couldn't sit back and watch this innocent kid die. I thought I had more time before the enemy arrived. I made the decision to move without proper intel." He turned his face away from her.

"Oh, Luke." Tears welled, but she held them at bay. "Look at me."

Slowly, he did.

"You were trying to save a child." She kissed his eyelids, his forehead. "I'm so sorry."

He was opening up and talking about something real, allowing her to share in his pain—pain that was still raw after all these years.

Maybe they could go back. Correct past mistakes. Maybe she could trust that what was happening between them was real and could last this time.

Or was history the best predictor of the future?

LUKE HAD NEVER spoken about the details of the day he was captured and Jared was killed. Not to his counselor. Not to his family. Not to anyone. "As soon as I grabbed the kid, I ran toward the tree line. All hell broke loose. I got shot before I made it to cover. Jared came running out, firing his weapon wildly. The guys came after him. I'd told them to leave me no matter what happened. They didn't. I should've known better because I would've done the same thing."

"Oh, baby, it wasn't your fault. You didn't have to go through that alone," Julie said.

Her words soothed his aching heart. He'd kept those feelings bottled up for so long, he felt as if he might explode some days. Time healed physical wounds—he had proof on his thigh where the bullet had penetrated him—but emotional scars were a totally different story. Did they ever really heal?

She whispered a few more words that brought a sense of calm over him. For the first time in a long time, he felt the dagger that had been stabbed through his heart had loosened. The constant hollow feeling in his chest was beginning to fill with hope and light. Surprisingly, it didn't feel like a betrayal.

Her breath on his skin as she whispered soothing words brought him back to life.

Julie brought him back to life.

He took her in his arms, pulled her tightly into his chest and released tears of anger and frustration that had been bottled inside him far too long. "Losing my friends made me want to die, but losing Jared…that was the worst. That's why I couldn't talk about him."

"I'm glad you told me, Luke."

He turned away, the familiar feeling of shame washing over him. Luke Campbell didn't cry. Besides, if he looked into her eyes, would he see pity there? He wouldn't be able to stand it if he'd let her down, too.

"Look at me."

Was it confirmation that had him needing to see her? Wiping away the moisture that had gathered under his eyes, he turned and faced her.

Her gaze was steady, reassuring and filled with compassion, not pity. "It's not weakness that makes you feel emotion, Luke Campbell."

"You didn't grow up with brothers," he mumbled, half joking, trying to lighten the mood. Although he'd never cried in front of his brothers, he knew deep down inside that they wouldn't fault him for it. The Campbell family always had each other's backs. Trusting outside of their circle was the difficult part. Luke thought about the soldier he'd helped train who never came home. Luke had nearly died overseas. The torture he'd endured felt like just deserts. But Luke had survived a bullet wound and weeks in enemy camp. He'd lived despite the odds. He finally picked himself up, decided to come home and waited until he could escape. And yet, there wasn't a day that went by he wouldn't exchange his life for any one of the men he'd fought alongside.

Luke had spent a year in counseling before he could round up the courage to visit Jared's parents in Spokane, Washington. He drove his truck from the family ranch. The closer he got, the heavier his arms felt.

"The people who tortured you were savage. Being sad or hurt because you had to watch people you love die doesn't make you weak. Compassion separates good people from bad," she said, cutting into Luke's heavy thoughts. "Think that monster chasing us cares about the lives he wrecks? Ignoring your pain and not facing it makes it grow into a beast."

There was truth in her words and they resonated with Luke. "Guess I never thought of it that way. I thought I had to be the strong one. Hold everything inside."

"Well, you don't. I'm here for you, Luke. You can't always go around protecting me and disappearing. I wanted to be there for you before."

"What about now?" He arched a brow and tried his level best not to reveal how much her answer mattered to him.

"How could I not? My feelings for you haven't changed, but I have."

"Because of me."

"No matter what happens between us, I will always be there for you as a friend."

Hurt darkened his brown eyes, but he blinked it away, kissing her pulse at the base of her neck. He smoothed his palm over her flat belly. "Have I told you how much I like this?"

"Yes."

"Or how beautiful you are first thing in the morning?"

His lips brushed the soft skin of her throat, leading to her pink lips.

"Yes."

"Or how seeing you in my old AC/DC shirt nearly drove me wild the other night?"

"That one I haven't heard."

"It did." He nibbled her earlobe.

"Do you forgive yourself yet?"

"I'm a work in progress." He palmed her breast. Her nipple pebbled in his hand.

Her fingers tunneled into his hair, and she gently pulled a fistful.

He pressed his forehead to hers. "So, where does that leave us exactly?"

"I don't know yet." She paused a beat. "We're a work in progress."

"Sounds fair." He could live with that.

The sounds of his cell vibrating cut into the moment. He glanced at the screen. Jenny from his forensic evidence team was on the line. "I better take this." He kissed her again. On the lips this time. The taste of coffee lingered on her mouth.

"Sorry it's taken so long to get back to you, but we have a match on the shoe print," Jenny said.

"Great. What did you find?"

"This particular shoe isn't cheap. It's handcrafted by—get this—an old man who lives in a small village in Italy. They don't sell a lot because each pair costs over a thousand dollars."

"Not something many men would spend money on." Which didn't exactly rule Rick out, or Chad, for that matter. Luke made a mental note to circle back around to Chad. The phone number he'd given Luke for his stepbrother had turned out to be a dead end.

Was Chad covering for his half brother?

He didn't appear to like Rick. But appearances weren't everything. And blood was blood. Maybe the two were closer than Chad had let on.

More questions that needed answers entered Luke's mind. He needed to interview the young guy's coworkers. See if he could dig up more about the relationship between him and his sibling. "So, what you're saying is whoever owns this shoe has serious funds?"

"Exactly. You didn't find anything missing from the crime scene this time, did you?"

"No. He must not've had time. The trinkets he really likes to take can't be bought. This guy likes hair and scalp."

"We knew that much." Most ritual killers held on to whatever piece of their victim they'd taken in order to relive the event for weeks, months.

"On the shoes, not many people can afford these babies. Fine Italian leather. Good news for us is they leave a specific impression."

"I'd like to see for myself. Maybe I need to dust off my

passport." Disappearing and taking Julie with him had crossed Luke's mind more than once. He needed a minute to sort through all the information he'd gained in the past forty-eight hours.

A chortle came across the line. "You wish. The boss isn't sending you to Italy to check on shoes."

Luke thanked her and ended the call.

He'd especially considered going on the run with Julie until this whole mess blew over and Rob was behind bars. Problem was, Luke was the FBI's best chance at catching Rob. And there were already too many innocent women being butchered in the meantime. Now that this had become personal, the body count was rising. Rob had promised more. In his haste, he would make a mistake. He had to.

Julie had disappeared into the bathroom, returning wearing nothing more than one of his T-shirts and her underwear.

He pulled her onto his lap and kissed the back of her neck.

Luke had a problem. Protocol said he should leave her at the safe house, guarded. Yet, Rob had tricked Luke before and almost got away with abducting her. He couldn't risk that happening twice. Keeping her with him was the only option.

"We have a serious problem to take care of before we leave," he said to her.

She turned enough for him to see her brow furrowed. "What is it, Luke?"

He spun her around to face him and then kissed her. She tasted minty and like dark-roasted coffee. "I can't get enough of you."

Julie broke into a laugh as she lowered her hand to his already straining erection. "Is that so?"

He nodded, groaning as her fingers curled around his shaft and gently squeezed.

"Good. Because I'm not done with you, either."

## Chapter Twelve

Luke had reluctantly finished dressing and kissed Julie again before moving into the living room to check his laptop.

He'd received an email from Nick stating that the background check on Chad's mother came up clean. In fact, he and his mother had been on vacation together during one of the murders. Nick was still digging around to find an address for Rick.

Luke glanced up from the screen, and his heart flipped when he saw her. She looked as beautiful as ever. No, more. Her hair was pulled back in a ponytail. A few loose strands framed her face. Her body was amazing. He already knew he'd never get enough of exploring her sensual curves. He logged off before that body of hers got him going again. "Ready?"

She nodded.

He led her to the elevator and then the truck. Backup was all around them, and yet an uneasy feeling still sat in his stomach like bad food.

Of course, every time he walked out the door with Julie he disliked the feeling of being exposed. With one hand on her back and the other ready to grip his weapon, he kept a watchful eye on everyone who passed by.

Rob had succeeded in making Luke paranoid. But the

stakes had never been higher. The thought of what Rob would do to Julie if he got his hands on her... Luke couldn't go there.

A visual scan of the garage yielded nothing.

One of his guys stood in the corner, smoking. He had arm-sleeve tattoos and wore a rock-band T-shirt with ripped jeans. Luke glanced at him for confirmation. The undercover agent popped his chin, giving the all-clear sign.

The restaurant would be easy enough to find using GPS. Upscale places like the DeBleu usually required their waiters to show up at lunch to taste the evening's specials and prepare their stations, so if Luke was lucky the staff would be there.

Traffic was light enough to make it to Addison in twenty minutes. For most of the ride, he filled Julie in on the shoe print left at the crime scene and the news he'd received from his brother. After parking and scanning the lot, Luke double-checked the notes he'd made on his phone.

Inside, a man wearing a long white apron greeted them. "I'm sorry. We're not open for lunch."

"We're not here for food." Luke flashed his badge and introduced himself. "I'd appreciate a moment of your time."

A look of shock crossed the guy's blond features. He introduced himself as Stephen before saying, "Of course."

"I'd like to speak to you about Chad Devel. Is he here by any chance?"

"Afraid not. He's not on the schedule tonight. Why? Did he do something wrong?"

"No." Luke smiled to ease the guy's tension. "I was hoping to ask him a few routine questions while I was here. Did he work on the night of the twenty-second?"

"Let's see. I worked that night. It was a Thursday. Decent night for tips." He glanced right as he recalled the date. "Yeah, he was here."

"Can you verify he was here the entire evening?"

"Yes. We give twenty minutes for dinner break, so he was here all night."

"Doesn't seem like much time to eat."

"I've found if I give longer, they disappear and don't always come back. Twenty minutes is enough time to eat. They put their order in before break, and when it comes up, they hit the back room," he said defensively.

Luke nodded as if he understood, to gain sympathy. "Is Chad a good sous chef?"

"He took a while to train, but once he got the hang of it, he's done all right," Stephen said.

"I hate to ask this question, but is he trustworthy?" Luke figured he'd get more information if he buddied up with Stephen.

"He wouldn't still work here if he wasn't."

"This is a beautiful place," Julie said.

Pride flashed behind Stephen's eyes as he looked at Luke. "You should bring her back for dinner sometime. On me."

"I appreciate it. I'll keep that in mind." Luke paused for effect. "Mind if I speak with a couple of your employees while I'm here?"

"Sure. Which ones?" Being treated with respect seemed to be the trick to getting Stephen to open up.

"Tony and Angie. Are they around by any chance?"

"Unfortunately, only one still works here. Angie quit last night in the middle of her shift."

"Sounds like she left you in the lurch."

"You wouldn't believe. I got it covered, but what a disaster."

"I can only imagine. These kids have no idea what real responsibility is like."

Stephen gave a nod of approval for the solidarity.

"Do you happen to have a good address for Tony?"

"Sure. Give me a minute, and I'll check employee records." The man made a move toward the kitchen but stopped and turned. "Would either of you like a cup of coffee? Tea?"

Luke glanced toward Julie, who smiled and shook her head.

"We're okay. Thanks."

Satisfied, Stephen disappeared toward the sounds of clanking pans.

Quick surveillance of the restaurant showed nothing unusual. Luke hadn't expected to find anything out of the ordinary, but experience had taught him he could never be sure when a case was about to break wide open. And they usually did so in an instant. Gut instinct was honed from years of experience. And his rarely failed.

He moved to block more of Julie with his large frame as they waited for Stephen to return.

The blond manager exploded from the kitchen with a piece of paper in his hands. "I'm sorry."

Luke's body went on full alert—ready for whatever was about to come his way. His hand instinctively went to the handle of his gun resting on his hip.

"It seems word got out you were here interrogating me. Tony ran out the back door." He jogged toward them and stuck out the piece of paper.

The roar of a motorcycle engine sounded from the parking lot. Luke muttered a curse and turned tail after taking the address.

"Thanks for the information," he said out of the side of

his mouth with a dry smile. "And if I were interrogating you, you'd know it."

He winked, motioning Julie to follow.

Camera phone ready, he snapped a pic of the motorcycle as it turned right out of the parking lot. He sent the photo to Detective Garcia.

The guy's address was on the sheet of paper. If it was legit, then Luke would wait for him at his house. Running was never a sign of innocence. This guy was doing something wrong. Luke needed to figure out what.

From the parking lot to Tony's apartment was a three-minute ride. Luke didn't figure the guy would be stupid enough to go home, but that was exactly what he'd done. The motorcycle sat in the parking lot near the address the restaurant manager had provided.

Either this guy was small-time or just stupid. Luke's experience had taught him to reserve judgment until he spoke to someone.

The two-story stucco apartment building had roughly thirty units total.

Tony's was on the second floor.

"I want you so close I can feel your breath," he said to Julie.

She nodded, her wide amber eyes signaling her fear.

"We'll be fine," he reassured her, then ascended the concrete-and-metal stairs at the end of the building.

"You don't think it's him?"

"No. Something's up. But I don't think it's Rob. Believe me, we wouldn't be going in without backup if I thought for a second he'd be here, but this guy's scared, and I need to find out what he's hiding."

She was so close he could hear her blow out a breath behind him. His reassurance seemed to ease her tension a notch below panic. Good. He liked being able to calm her fears.

Besides, what he'd said was absolute gospel. He'd never knowingly face down Rob with her present and without any reinforcements. There was a slight possibility that Rob was working with someone else. If not directly, then someone could be covering his tracks. That someone could be his brother or Chad's friends. The circumstantial evidence against Rick was mounting. A rich dad might do anything to shield his son. Especially if the boy had been abused. But the fact Rick grew up in California worked against them logistically, Luke thought as he rapped on the door. "FBI. Open up."

Silence.

"Open up or I'll break down the door. Either way, we're going to talk. Your choice." Luke didn't have a warrant, so there was no way he would force entry. But the guy behind the door didn't know that. It was a gamble.

The door swung open.

Taking a risk paid off.

A twentysomething guy stood there, wide-eyed. His hand trembled on the knob. "Can I help you?"

"I'm Special Agent Campbell, and I'd like to ask you a few questions."

"Okay." His five-foot-ten frame blocked the opening.

"May we come in?"

"No, sir." The guy's voice shook, too.

"I'm not here to bust you. I need answers. As long as you cooperate, we're good." He intentionally used a calm tone.

"Okay. Did I do something wrong?" The door didn't budge.

"Not that I know of. At least, not yet. Obstructing an ongoing murder investigation is a serious charge."

"Holy crap." He shook his head. "I didn't kill anyone."

"I know you didn't." Luke paused to give the young man a minute to think. "But you might be able to stop a crime."

The guy glanced around. "Can't you ask me right here?"

"There anything inside I need to be worried about?"

"No."

"Are you lying to me?"

"No, sir."

"Then why are you afraid to open the door?"

"I'm not, sir." He glanced around nervously and cracked the door. "Is that good?"

"Better." Luke felt more comfortable being able to see inside. "Do you know Chad Devel?"

"Yes." A mix of relief and apprehension played across his features. "He's a buddy of mine from work."

"You two close?"

"Somewhat. Why? Is he okay?" Concern knitted his dark bushy eyebrows together. He was another one who looked as if he'd stepped off an Abercrombie & Fitch ad. Tall, thin, with thick hair and a sullen look on his face.

"Everything's fine. We're trying to make sure it stays that way."

"Is someone after him?" He scrubbed his hands across the light stubble on his chin.

"Do you know his brother?"

"Rick? Yeah, sure. Haven't seen him in a while, though. He hasn't been coming around to Chad's place."

Interesting. Chad had given them the impression he didn't hang out with his brother.

Guess he'd lied. Luke didn't like liars. "When's the last time you saw him at his brother's?"

"Been a couple of months. Why? Did Rick do something wrong?"

That put him in the Metroplex for a few of the killings. "No. You expecting him to?"

The guy wiped his palms down the front of his pants. "He seems the type. I mean, he hangs around with us but doesn't party. Doesn't say much, either. He's sort of creepy."

"Couldn't he just be straitlaced?"

"That's what I thought at first, too. But then he showed up one night—one look at him and I could tell he was on something."

"Drugs?"

Tony nodded. "Except Chad swore his brother didn't partake, you know."

Luke didn't, but he nodded anyway. "I didn't think Rick lived around here."

"Yeah. He's got a place near Chad."

"Addison Circle?"

Tony nodded. "I've never been to his place, though."

"I didn't realize the two of them were so close."

"Chad's kind of protective of him. Feels sorry for him. Said he had a bad childhood or something."

"Their dad?"

"Nah. His mom. She's some kind of freak, from what Chad says. He doesn't really like his brother. He pities the guy."

Luke didn't see that one coming. Rick fit the profile. His age was on the money. Learning he had an estranged mother made Luke wonder if that had anything to do with the bleach. He cleansed his "projects" then tortured them. This was one angry and twisted guy. Of course, abuse did bad things to a kid's brain. He certainly had the income to be able to afford expensive Italian shoes, or they could've been a present.

He exchanged a look with Julie. She was clearly thinking the same thing.

Except Luke's killer knew the area well. "How long has his brother been living here?"

"On and off for a year, I think."

"Where else does he live?"

"He goes back and forth between here and California now that he got kicked out of medical school."

Luke practically had the wind knocked out of him.

Rob cut his victims with medical precision. Rick had been in medical school? He'd have access to the kind of tools Rob used. "How long did you say he's been here?"

"This time? A year."

"What do you mean by 'this time'?"

"Oh. He came here for high school. His dad shipped him off to an all-male boarding school to get him away from his mother or something. Sent him to Dallas so he'd be close to Chad."

Spending his high-school years here would definitely give him insight into the area. "You have Rick's address?"

"No. Like I said, I've never been to his place. I just know it's close to Chad's."

"You planning on leaving the area anytime soon?"

"No, sir."

"Good. I expect to be able to find you if I have more questions."

"Yes, sir."

"And if you run from me next time, I'll haul your butt to jail. Understood?"

"Yes, sir."

Luke led Julie out the door.

"Chad wasn't exactly honest with us yesterday, was he?" she asked in a whisper.

"Nope."

"We find him and we get our killer, don't we?" Her tone was like a line that had been pulled so taut, it was about to break.

"Looks that way," he said calmly.

"So are we heading to Chad's place?" Her voice hitched on the last word.

"No."

"Why not?" She whirled on him.

"I told you that I wouldn't risk your safety. We can't go back alone." He urged her to keep walking. Truth was, Rob could be watching them right now.

Reality dawned on her as her eyes widened. "Oh. Right. *He* could be there."

Luke followed her down the stairs and to the truck. He opened her door for her and helped her in. "He's near. And I'd venture to guess either he or Chad drives a gray sedan."

She gasped as she buckled her seat belt. "The car that followed us?"

"I didn't believe it was a coincidence then. And I sure don't now." Luke took his seat on the driver's side and scanned the lot. "I need to find a good place for you to hide while I pay our friend another visit."

Her hand on his arm normally brought heat where she touched. This time was different. He could feel her shaking. The idea of being away from her didn't do good things to the acid already churning in his gut. On balance, there was no other choice. Under the circumstances, there was only one option he could consider. Luke fished his cell from his pocket and tapped on his brother-in-law's name in his contacts. "Riley, are you on shift right now?"

"Yes, but I can break for lunch anytime. What's up?"

"I need a favor."

"Anything."

Luke picked a meeting spot halfway between them,

which was fifteen minutes away, and ended the call. He turned to Julie as he started the ignition. "You okay with hanging out with Riley for a while?"

"Of course. It'll be good to see him." Her eyes told him a different story.

"What is it?"

"Nothing." She bit her bottom lip.

Lying?

"You know I'm going to be fine." He glanced in her direction as he pulled out of the parking lot and headed north. They'd agreed on a spot at the border where Plano met Dallas on the Tollway.

She didn't respond.

"I don't take unnecessary risks."

"I know," she said quietly. "This guy is…bad."

"I've dealt with worse," he said, trying his best to sound convincing. Luke meandered onto the Tollway and headed north. He took the Parker Road exit and pulled into the strip shopping center. He hadn't noticed the voice mail registered on his phone. Luke listened to the message from Nick, confirming what he'd just learned—Rick Camden had flunked out of medical school. Nick was working on getting a current address. Luke hit the end button and stuffed the phone in his pocket.

Riley waited in his squad car.

"Give me a minute to get Riley up to speed, okay?" he asked Julie.

She nodded.

He didn't like how quiet she was being, especially since seeing the concern in her eyes.

With his hand on the door handle, he paused. "You know I'm coming back to get you in an hour, right?"

It was then he noticed the tears that had been welling in her eyes. He came around to her side of the truck and pulled her into his arms. She burrowed into his chest, trembling. "Be careful."

"I'll be fine."

He lifted her chin until her gaze met his. He thumbed away her tears. "Look at me. I promise I'll be back in an hour or two. You're not getting rid of me that easy." He winked.

Her nod was tentative.

"I give you my word." He paused for emphasis. "You believe me, right?"

"Yes." Her chin lifted a little higher.

"That's my girl."

He tucked her into the passenger seat of Riley's SUV, the standard issue for patrol in Plano, and asked his brother-in-law to step out for a minute.

Riley did.

"You need a heads-up on this one. This guy's the worst."

"I've been watching the bulletins. Plus, we got information at briefing. We have a lot of eyes looking for him."

"Then you know what he's capable of."

Riley nodded, an ominous look settling over his features.

"Keep her safe." Luke didn't like leaving her, not even with one of the few men he'd trust with his own life. "And be careful. This guy doesn't care about the badge you're wearing. Won't stop him."

"Got it. You, too. Your sister would kill me if anything happened to you on my watch." Riley's attempt at humor succeeded in lightening the somber mood.

Luke couldn't help but crack a smile. "I wouldn't want to be on the wrong side of a postpartum woman like Meg."

"Good thing I love her."

Luke had already started toward his truck.

"Watch your back, man," Riley said.

Luke waved, turned to circle around the vehicle and give Julie another kiss goodbye. "I'll see you after lunch. Save me a taco."

# Chapter Thirteen

"It's great to see you again, Riley." Julie tried to distract herself from the fact that Luke was about to face down a ruthless killer. *Possibly* face down, she corrected. After all, the guy might not be home. And, although the evidence was condemning, there was no guarantee they were on the right track. Plus, he was going to see Chad, not Rick.

Her nerves were bundled tight. She feared they'd snap if someone so much as said boo.

"You, too," Riley said.

"Congratulations on two fronts. Getting married and I heard you're a new dad. I bet he's beautiful." Any other time she'd be interested in hearing all the details about the boy's birth and first few weeks in the world, but all she could focus on now was Luke's safety.

"He is. Keeping us on our toes." Riley smiled as he cut across the lot and parked in front of the Tex-Mex restaurant she remembered was his favorite.

"I haven't been here in ages. I miss the food."

"It's almost a sin to live anywhere near here and not visit Eduardo's."

She smiled at his visible display of outrage. "How's Meg?"

"Good. Becoming a mother suits her."

Julie got out of the SUV and met him around the front

of the hood. She couldn't help but check out the people around her warily. Would there ever come a time when she didn't fear someone was watching? Riley stared at her, one hand on the butt of his gun. "Everything okay?"

"Yeah. It's just I always feel like he's close." She shivered.

"You've been through a lot. I can't blame you for being spooked. You want to go somewhere else to eat? Meg's home. I can take you there."

"And make you miss out on Eduardo's enchiladas? Are you crazy?" She tried to shake off the feeling. "Besides, I don't want to get in the way of Meg bonding with her new baby. And I want to hear about Hitch."

Riley followed her inside. As they waited for a table, he leaned toward her and whispered, "Three of my fellow officers are outside."

"I didn't see anyone else." And she'd looked carefully.

"Exactly. They're in plain clothes. Out of sight. But they're there. I called in a few favors after my conversation with Luke."

The hostess greeted them and led them toward their table in between no less than four tables full of uniformed officers from Dallas and Richardson. She guessed it was true what they said about law enforcement sticking together.

She smiled. "More favors?"

He nodded as he took his seat. "Couldn't have Luke worrying about you while he did his job, now, could I?"

Julie let out her breath, realizing for the first time her fingers had been practically clamped together in a death grip. "Thank you."

"He called in for backup. You know that, right?" Riley said, his tone serious.

"I hadn't thought of it, but you're right. Of course he would do that."

"You're safe. He's doing his job. And he's the best. He's survived much worse. A jerk like Rob isn't going to get the best of Luke."

"You're right again." She wished she shared his confidence. Fear of losing Luke rippled through her. If not by Rob's hands, then by some trigger that made Luke shut down again. She didn't want to admit to herself how deeply her feelings ran. She'd sworn no one would have that kind of power over her again. Her feelings for him were resurfacing, but that didn't mean things would magically work out this time.

The waiter came to take their orders. He placed a bowl of chips and salsa on the table.

Riley picked up a chip and dipped it in the salsa. "You okay?"

"I guess. Everything's happening so fast. This guy. He's everywhere but nowhere."

"Everyone's looking for him."

"Between that and being this close to Luke again, I'm confused. Scared."

"He hasn't been the same for the past four years."

"But he picked up his life and moved on. I know he's dated other people."

"After a few years we tried to set him up. Lucy had a friend on the force she thought might help bring him out of his funk."

A jealous twinge fired through her.

"Didn't work. He wouldn't...didn't... She liked him, but they ended up friends. The relationship was purely platonic."

"I'm sure there were others." She didn't lift her gaze to meet his. Instead, she toyed with the chip in her fingers.

"True. Over time. I heard."

"You didn't meet them?"

"No. He never brought them to the ranch."

Her heavy heart filled with light.

Food arrived.

They smiled at the waiter and thanked him.

"Thanks for telling me that." It didn't solve all their problems, but it did ease the sting of how easy it seemed for him to walk away before.

"I just hate to see two people who fit so well together go through what you two have."

"When did you become such a hopeless romantic?"

"Having a baby has weakened me," he joked. He pulled his phone from his shirt pocket and opened a picture then handed it to her.

"Is that him?" Hitch had the Campbell family's dark hair. Brown eyes. Dimpled smile. If her heart could've melted in her chest right then and there, it would've.

Riley practically beamed.

Julie smiled back at him. "One look at that angel's face and I can see why you changed."

She handed the phone to him, took a chip, dipped it in salsa and leaned closer. "Thank you for telling me what you did before. About me and Luke. It helps. But now I'd like to hear more about that beautiful wife and boy of yours."

LUKE HAD CALLED for backup on his way south on the Tollway. Chad wasn't at work. With it being midday, Luke figured there was a good chance the guy was still asleep. He already knew Chad liked to party on his days off.

A squad car was already parked in the lot when Luke arrived. He thanked the SWAT officers and led the way to Chad's place.

Three raps on the door, and he yelled, "FBI. Open up."

Noises came from the other side of the door. Did Chad have company? Rick wouldn't go down easy.

"Might be hot," he told the pair of SWAT officers flanking him.

They stepped aside, following his lead.

He pounded the door with his fist this time. "I hear you in there, Chad. Open up."

A minute later, the door flew open. Chad stood there in his boxer shorts. A young woman, barely clothed, curled up on the couch, hugging a pillow.

"What can I do for you?"

Luke stepped inside and grabbed Chad by the neck, slamming his back against the door. "You lied to me."

Chad shook his head, wincing.

The girl screamed.

"You want to start all over, and tell me the truth this time?"

Chad shook his head. His face turned blood red. "Lawyer."

"Innocent people don't need lawyers, Chad." Luke loosened his grip enough for Chad to speak.

"Dude, I don't know what you're talking about."

"You told me you didn't know where Rick was. Is he here right now?"

Chad shook his head.

"You better not be lying to me. Mind if the officers double-check?"

"Go ahead. I swear he isn't here."

The officers split up, guns leveled.

"Why did you lie to me, Chad?" Luke gripped the guy's neck a little tighter.

"Who told you I lied?"

"I visited your job and asked a few questions. You and

Rick are close, aren't you? What? Didn't you think I'd check up on your story?"

Chad shook his head, gasping for air.

Luke eased up enough for Chad to breathe.

"Stop. You're hurting him," the girl pleaded, hugging the pillow tighter.

"You want a trip downtown?" Luke didn't move his arm from across Chad's chest and neck, but he glanced at her.

"No."

"No, what?"

"No, sir."

"Then stay put and keep quiet." Luke turned his attention back to Chad, keeping the girl in his peripheral view. "Your brother have a medical problem?"

"He's diabetic."

Luke bit back a curse.

"Clear," one of the officers said.

The other repeated the word a few minutes later. They returned to the living room at the same time. One held up a shoe with a gloved hand.

"This the item you're looking for, Special Agent Campbell?"

Luke examined the shoe without touching it, keeping one elbow on Chad's chest. "This is it." He leveled his gaze at Chad.

"What does my shoe have to do with anything?"

"Still playing stupid, Chad?"

"I seriously don't know what you're talking about."

"This your shoe?"

"Yes."

"Then you just bought yourself a trip downtown." Luke turned to the officers. "Gentlemen."

"Hold on a sec. What's going on?" The young man looked genuinely confused.

Luke had to give it to Chad: the guy played stupid to an art form. Either that or he really was in the dark about his half brother's illegal activity.

"This shoe is rare, isn't it, Chad?"

"Yeah. So what?"

"This print was found at the scene of two murders."

The color drained from Chad's face.

"Gruesome murders. Someone's chopping up women with a surgical saw." Luke loosened his grip so Chad wouldn't pass out. Instead, he sank to the floor.

"My dad gave me those shoes for Christmas three years ago."

"Let me guess—he gave your brother the same pair."

"Half brother."

"So I'm reminded."

"And the answer is yes." Sitting on the floor, Chad looked small and devastated. Both hands gripped his head as he leaned his face toward his knees.

"You've been covering for your half brother, haven't you?"

"Yeah, because I feel sorry for the guy."

"Why?"

"His mom is crazy. The only reason Dad left my mom for her was because he didn't want Rick growing up alone. I suspected she did cruel…*things*…to him, but he never talked about it."

"What things?"

Tears spilled onto his cheeks. "I don't know. Torture, I guess. He'd show up with bruises all over his body. Dad would send him here because he couldn't go back to school looking like that. Even as a kid I knew he didn't get them from playing. He wasn't into sports, either. He was pretty brainy. He'd sit in the corner of my room and rock his head back and forth. Sometimes, it'd take days for him to acknowledge me. Whatever Bev did to him was awful. His mom was a twisted bitch."

"That why he soaks his victim's clothes in bleach?"

Chad dry heaved. "I'm sorry. I didn't know. According to my mom, Bev threatened to ruin my dad's reputation and that's why he left us. She manipulated and blackmailed him. I can only imagine what else she did to Rick."

"Or cuts out pieces of their hair and scalps?"

"I would've turned him in myself if I'd…"

Luke bent down to Chad's level. "Where does he live?"

Chad stood, moved in front of the door and pointed to a building across the parking lot. "Right there. Number two hundred and two."

"You listen to me carefully. Your sick bastard of a brother is after someone I love. You run into him, you better tell him this for me. He just made this personal. I'll see him in hell before I let him hurt the people I care about."

Chad nodded slowly.

Luke lowered his voice when he said, "You see him? Tell him he's not the only one who can play games."

He turned toward the officers. "Anything worth running him downtown for here?"

They shook their heads. "If he had anything, he got rid of it before he let us in."

"Mind taking his statement and filing the report?"

"Not at all," one of the officers replied.

"I owe you one." Luke needed to get out of there.

An ominous feeling had settled over him, and all he could think about was getting to Julie.

## Chapter Fourteen

Luke updated his report, put out a BOLO—a Be On the Lookout alert—and entered Rick's address into the system with a request for a warrant to search the premises. If all went well, he'd be back at Rick's in an hour, and Julie would be safe. Heck, as long as he was wishing, Rick would be locked up before she finished lunch.

Before Luke left the parking lot, he rounded up the pair of officers and headed toward the apartment across the lot. He rapped on the door several times and listened. No one answered, and the place was dead quiet. Knowing the way this guy operated, he'd watched the events unfold at his half brother's and was long gone.

No answer. No warrant. They'd have to come back.

After thanking the officers, Luke hopped on the Tollway and headed toward Plano.

Seeing a half-dozen officers surround Julie when he arrived at the restaurant lowered his blood pressure to a reasonable level.

Her face lit up when he walked into the room, and his muscles relaxed another notch.

"How'd it go?" She threw her arms open and turned her face to the side slightly.

He'd already seen the tears of relief. He held her until she stopped shaking and kissed the top of her head.

The waiter interrupted, taking Luke's order before disappearing into the kitchen.

Julie took a seat next to him as he turned his attention toward Riley. "I owe you one, man."

"I'll start a tab," he joked, no doubt an attempt to lighten the mood.

Luke smiled his gratitude. "We need a new place to stay. Think you can help out with that?" Staying on the move was their best chance.

"I know of a place. I'd like to keep you inside my city limits. You good with that?"

"Absolutely." Luke figured the best place for them was close to family in case he needed a quick place to stash Julie. Besides, with half of Plano P.D. watching out for them, he'd sleep better at night.

"Find anything useful on your shopping trip?" Riley glanced around, using code on the off chance someone was listening.

Luke nodded. "Wasn't bad. Call you later with the details?"

"Sure. Sounds like you identified what you were looking for."

"It's him. No doubt in my mind."

Officers stood, one by one, and gave a nod toward Riley's table.

Luke shook their hands. After eating and thanking his brother-in-law again, Luke helped Julie into the truck and waved goodbye.

"I'll get back to you with the address we talked about," Riley shouted before he drove off.

Before Luke could put the truck in Drive, he got the text he'd been hoping for. "I have a warrant to search Rick's place. We're heading back to Addison."

Julie's gaze widened. "You found out where he lives?"

"Yeah. And it's right across the parking lot from Chad. I've requested uniformed officers to assist. There'll be plenty of backup. Plus, I already know he's not there."

"How can you be sure?"

"He's too smart, for one. He knows we're onto him. Plus, with the location of his place across from Chad's, he's been watching everything that goes on at his brother's. Chad's most likely telling his brother all about our conversation. The shoe print found at the scene of the murders belongs to a shoe given to Rick for Christmas three years ago, according to his brother."

"Is it safe?"

"I don't know what we'll find at his place, maybe nothing, but I'm one hundred percent certain he won't be there. If I had any doubt, I wouldn't bring you." He glanced at her as he navigated the truck out of the parking lot and headed toward the on-ramp. "You good with this? I can always drop you at the station until we're done."

"No," she said quickly. "I want to go with you. It was agony being in the restaurant without you. Not knowing if something had happened… I'd rather be there."

Luke knew exactly how she felt. Even with officers surrounding her the entire time he was away, he'd had an uneasy feeling. Rick was *that* cunning.

His phone chirped, indicating a text had arrived. Luke retrieved his cell from his pocket and handed it to Julie.

She studied the screen. "It's an address from Riley."

"Looks like we have a place to stay tonight."

"I guess there's no chance we can go back to where we were before?" She sounded resigned to be on the run.

"It's best to stay on the move. That's the only way to keep ahead of Rick. Besides, I don't want to jeopardize my friends any more than I have to." The situation was no doubt wearing her down. She seemed determined to keep fighting and hold her own. Her innate survival instincts would help keep her alive.

Problem was, this case was escalating fast. Too fast.

They arrived back at Rick's apartment before the police. Luke parked the truck and palmed his weapon. He surveyed the parking lot for a gray sedan but found nothing matching the description.

"What did you find out from Chad?"

"It's him. Rick is our guy. In addition to the shoe match, Chad also confirmed his brother is diabetic."

"The orange juice that was left out at my client's house."

"Exactly. Plus, there's a history of mental instability in the family."

"His dad?"

"Mom. The reason Dad left Chad's mom to be with the other woman was because he didn't trust her to be alone with his son. Sounds like she held Rick over his head, too. If news of that got out, it could threaten his professional reputation."

"Sounds bad. What kind of person would hurt their own child?"

"Might explain why Rob chops off his victims' heads. He's trying to make his mother pay."

Color drained from Julie's face. "That's so sad."

"Chad believes there was torture involved, but he didn't talk specifics."

"It's awful what human beings can do to one another."

"Not all kinds of love is good." Luke's had been poison when he'd returned from active duty. Or so he'd thought at the time. Took him a year and visits with a counselor to acknowledge he had the classic signs of post-traumatic stress disorder. The same shame he felt at not being able to save his brothers in arms resurfaced every time he heard Rick killed another innocent victim. Every part of Luke wanted to shut down again with the news. The past two years had been like reliving those early months all over again. Except now that he had Julie in his life again, he had even more to fight for to stay grounded and not let the situation get the best of him.

A dull ache pounded between his temples—a searing headache threatened. He remembered the killer ones he'd had four years ago. They'd almost split his head in two.

Other PTSD signs were returning, too.

Luke shoved them down deep. He had to catch Rick or risk losing everything again.

A pair of squad cars parked in front of Luke's truck. He was informed the SWAT team would be arriving to assist.

"He's clever, so don't expect much," he warned the officers. "We might find a shoe match to crime scenes." He showed them the picture.

A minivan pulled up, the doors opened and a team of SWAT officers spilled out. Luke greeted them and pointed toward Rick's door. "Where can she stay while we check things out?"

"In the squad car with Officer Haines," Officer Melton said.

The SWAT officers took position with the Hammer—the key to the city known for its ability to open all doors.

"One…two…three…" The officer who'd identified himself as the supervisor swung the Hammer, bursting through the lock. The door flew open.

One officer went right. One went left. The third took the middle. The officer with the Hammer held position at the door.

Not three minutes later, the supervisor gave the all clear.

Luke strode inside.

The place had a few pieces of modern furniture with a forty-two-inch flat-screen mounted on the wall. Since the space was open concept, Luke could see through to the kitchen with its stainless-steel appliances and granite countertops. In the bedroom, clothes were strewn and cabinets already half-empty. Clearly, Rick had made a hasty exit. Luke bit back a curse. He was so close he could almost feel the guy's presence still in the room. It was pure evil—not that he believed in that.

Besides, even if Rick were the devil incarnate, he'd still spend the rest of his days behind bars just like every other heinous criminal. If found guilty of multiple murders, he might just land an express ticket to death row, where he would be executed.

Luke turned the place over in twenty minutes while SWAT kept a close watch on the door and windows. There wasn't much to see except several cartons of orange juice in the fridge and empty bottles of insulin in the bathroom trash can. Proof he was a diabetic, but not necessarily a murderer. The empty bottles of hair-bonding glue in the trash were far more damning.

Maybe his evidence response team could find hair fibers linking Rick to one of the victims?

Luke updated the SWAT officers and called it in.

With Chad's statement, Rick qualified as a person of interest. It was enough to detain him for questioning. But if Luke had found something more concrete, even a drop of a victim's blood on Rick's clothing, he would feel better. Luke figured the guy would be smart enough to keep his tools somewhere else. But where? Surely not in his car.

The headache that had started in the car raged, causing a burning sensation in the backs of Luke's eyes.

A SWAT officer's body stiffened. "I see a guy who fits the description of the suspect watching us from across the parking lot. He's wearing a cobalt-blue sweatshirt and jeans."

Luke muttered a curse as he tore through the door, giving chase. He heard an officer say he would follow. Luke's full attention zeroed in on Sweatshirt.

The second Luke's foot hit concrete, Sweatshirt bolted. This was the closest Luke had been to the deranged killer. He could feel in his bones that this was Rick. A quick shot of adrenaline pulsed through him, powering his legs forward like rockets.

Rick disappeared in between buildings two hundred yards in front of Luke, but he kept pushing anyway. This might be his only hope of catching the bastard before he hurt someone else.

Anger and frustration coursed through Luke as he reached the buildings. He had to take a guess on the direction Rick went. His odds were fifty-fifty, and they were the best he'd had since this whole journey began two years ago. Luke didn't like it. He could not risk losing the guy this time.

"I'll take right," Luke shouted to the officer following without looking back. Acknowledgment came a second later through labored breaths.

Pushing forward, Luke ran until his sides cramped, his thighs burned and his lungs felt as if they might explode.

Shelving the pain, he ran some more.

He'd lost visual contact with Sweatshirt. The situation was becoming more hopeless by the second. A wave of desperation crashed through him. Then he saw something. A glimpse of cobalt blue sticking out from behind a car.

Luke charged toward it.

The piece of sweatshirt disappeared before Luke could get within twenty yards.

At least he was back on track.

The guy wasn't going to get far, if Luke had anything to say about it. He zigzagged through cars, pushing his body to the limit.

No way was Rick in better physical condition than Luke. If he could get close, he had no doubt he could overpower the guy or outrun him. All the advantage had gone to Rick so far. That was about to change. Luke knew who the bastard was, and so would the rest of the world as soon as Luke called Bill Hightower.

Heck, give him five minutes alone with the piece of human garbage and he'd do more than talk a confession out of him. He'd break him. Another five without the badge, and the man wouldn't walk out alive.

Another turn and Luke was closing in on him. He clenched his fists with the need to get his hands around the guy's neck.

Less than half a city block away, Luke pushed his legs further. Closing in at this speed, he'd be on top of Rick in a matter of minutes.

Before Luke could close the last bit of gap between them, Rick disappeared into a small crowd. There was a barbershop and a travel agency side by side at the place Luke had lost visual contact. After checking through the windows of both, it was clear from the commotion that Sweatshirt had ducked into the first.

A few seconds later, Luke burst through the doors of the barbershop. The few men inside looked startled.

"FBI." He flashed his badge. "There was a man who just ran through here."

Heads nodded confirmation.

"Where'd he go?"

Several men pointed toward what looked like a stockroom.

"Any employees in there I need to know about?" He drew his gun, leveled it.

"No. Everyone's out here," one of the employees said, already heading toward the front door.

"Where does that lead?" Luke asked as he stalked toward the back room.

"The alley."

Luke's hopes the place was sealed were dashed. "Everyone outside until someone with a badge tells you it's clear. Got it?" Luke muttered a curse and hauled himself toward the stockroom.

The door was open. He surveyed the room before entering. Even though it had been staged to look as if Rick had run out the back, he could be anywhere, ready to strike.

Luke took measured steps forward, keenly aware of the fact his guy might be getting away.

Underestimating Rick, believing the obvious, had gotten an officer killed already.

By the time Luke reached the alley, there was no sign of Rick. Didn't stop Luke from verifying what his eyes had already shown him. He doubled back and checked the stockroom one more time as he moved through it again. Luke slammed his fist against the wall and released a string of swearwords.

He pulled his composure together as he walked out front. "Everything's safe. Go inside and lock the doors."

"Thank you." The look of relief on the guy's face was fleeting as he scurried toward the stockroom.

Luke took a minute to get his bearings before making his way to the apartment.

Julie sat in the car of one of the SWAT officers.

"He knows the area well," Luke said to the supervisor, still heaving, trying to fill his lungs with air. Sweat rolled down his neck.

"We sent a couple of guys to back you up. They didn't get anywhere, either. We'll stick around until your team shows up to process the place."

After shaking his hand and thanking him for his help,

Luke walked Julie to the truck. He'd been so close to catching Rick. Anger railed through him. His hands shook. Head pounded.

If anyone else was hurt, how could he ever forgive himself?

A jolt of shame washed through him, and his body trembled.

"Luke? What's wrong?" Concern wrinkled Julie's forehead.

"Headache." He couldn't help but feel responsible for the deaths of the women so far. How the heck did he open up and talk about that? If he'd caught Rick two years ago, more than half a dozen lives would've been saved. Not to mention Julie wouldn't be in this mess.

The tremors started again as his headache dulled.

Fury ate at his gut as he fought the signs of PTSD overwhelming him.

## Chapter Fifteen

Luke checked outside the window onto the street. An officer was stationed in front of the house. Everything looked fine. And yet, everything felt off. Why?

*"This case,"* he said under his breath. There was a chill in the air and his warning systems had been tripped. Then again, his internal alarms had been firing rapidly ever since he'd chased Rick.

The small two-story in historic Plano was a good cover, he repeated silently for the hundredth time. One of Riley's friends would be driving past every ten minutes or so, in addition to the marked car on the street.

Luke prayed it would be enough.

He distracted himself by moving to the kitchen and fixing a light dinner of soup and BLTs for him and Julie, placing the meal on the island.

Julie descended the stairs. So beautiful. Her hair was still wet from the shower. Water beaded and rolled down her neck where he'd left a few love bites the night before. If anyone could keep him planted in reality, it was her.

"Feels so good to be clean," she said, taking a seat next to him.

"I can think of a few reasons to be dirty." He leaned toward her, touching elbows. The point of contact still spread heat through his arm. He'd never get tired of her.

A distant sound scarcely registered. Luke stiffened as he glanced toward the street. He raised his head as he scooped her up and instinctively headed for cover.

Tucking her behind the sofa, he set her down gently on the wooden floor. "Stay here until I say different."

Sounds of shouting rose from out front. A scuffle?

Before Luke could get to the window, the crack of a bullet split the air.

Luke immediately jumped into action, pulling his handgun from the waistband of his jeans and placing it in her palm. "Anyone you don't recognize comes through the door, aim and shoot. Ask questions later."

Her eyes were fearful, but she nodded, gripping the handle.

"And call 911. I'm heading out the back. Then I'll slip around the side. Find a safe spot and hide." Luke palmed his own weapon as he moved out the door and motioned for her to lock it behind him.

The porch lamp was on, lighting a small circle around the backyard. He didn't breathe easier until he heard the snick of the lock behind him. Back against the wall, he moved toward the street in the darkness.

The front-porch light was off and the street wasn't well lit. It would take a moment for his eyes to adjust to the pitch black surrounding him.

Luke moved to the black-and-white parked at the curb. No movement inside was not a good sign. He got close enough to see that the officer was slumped over. Luke released a string of curse words under his breath.

A flashback to the war assaulted him. *He watched helplessly as one of his best buddies was shot execution style.*

Luke raged against the memory. This was not Iraq. He was in Plano now, chasing a killer.

Fighting the instinct to run to the injured man, Luke

realized how vulnerable it would make him. How exposed Julie would be if anything happened to him.

Circling back, Luke texted his boss. Confirmation came quickly. More uniforms were on their way.

Rob was cunning. Luke had to give it to him. He was a determined killer.

But what the killer hadn't estimated was Luke's determination to stop him. He'd rather die than allow anything to happen to Julie. The thought of losing her again or, worse yet, having her taken from him detonated explosions of fire in his chest.

Running as fast as his legs would carry him, he reached the back door and knocked softly, not wanting to draw unwanted attention to himself. He pressed his back against the door and leveled his weapon, ready for an attack from the yard.

Anyone tried to cross that grass, Luke would be ready.

His chest squeezed when Julie didn't answer.

"Julie," he whispered, ever watchful of the threat around him. He'd break the door down in a heartbeat.

He knocked again. Still no answer.

Luke spun around and thrust his boot against the sweet spot in the door. It popped open. He wanted to scream her name but knew better.

Easing inside the kitchen, he crouched below the window line and moved through the space. One by one, he opened every door, checking for any sign of her.

The first floor was clear. Luke ascended the stairs, checking doors as he moved stealthily down the hallway toward the bedrooms.

The hall bath was empty, as were two secondary bedrooms.

A clank sounded downstairs.

Every instinct inside him said Rick was in the house.

Luke bit back another urge to call for Julie. He had to find her—now.

And he had to do it quietly.

He eased across the hardwood flooring, stepping around the places where the wood creaked, silently cursing Rick.

Tension pulled his shoulder blades taut. Where was she?

Where would she hide? Luke managed to make it to the walk-in closet in the master bedroom without making a sound.

However, someone was moving up the stairs and not being nearly as quiet. Rick? A cop?

Luke couldn't say for sure. All he could think about was getting to Julie. If she was still here. And that was a big *if*.

His grip on his handgun could crack concrete.

The door to the closet was ajar. The light off. Inside, there were two racks of clothing on either side. The back wall was made of deep shelving.

"Julie," he whispered.

A figure moved to his right.

Before he could get a good look, he had a body pinned against the wall and a hand over their mouth.

As soon as the body was flush with his, he realized Julie was in his arms, safe. He removed his hand.

"Is he here?" she whispered, rocketing into his arms.

"Someone's coming up the stairs. Don't figure we should wait to find out who." He tucked her behind his back and, weapon drawn, exited the closet.

A noise from the hall indicated that option was closed off.

They had two choices. Hide in the master bathroom and ambush the intruder and shoot at the first sign of movement. Or they could climb out the windows and get the hell out of there.

He double-checked that Julie was still armed, motioned

for her to keep her eyes glued to the door and cranked open the pane in the historic house.

There should be just enough room for Julie to slip out. The opening might not be big enough for Luke, but he could cover her until she could get to safety.

Luke touched Julie's arm to get her attention. The ledge was skinny, but she could scale it as long as she didn't look down. This wasn't the time to think about the fact she was afraid of heights.

Her wide eyes stared for a moment before she inhaled a deep breath, tucked the gun in the waistband of her jeans and climbed onto the ledge.

Luke kept his back to the window, facing the door. If Rob walked in, he'd be in for a surprise.

Daring a glance out the window a few minutes—minutes that ticked by like hours—later, he could see that she was safely on the ground, her weapon drawn just as he'd instructed. Pride swelled in his chest.

With Luke being significantly bigger than her, he'd have a much harder time squeezing his big frame through the opening.

As he jimmied his way outside, a noise in the hallway got his heart pumping. Right about that time, he realized he couldn't make forward progress. He tried to reposition so he could shift his weight toward the room and go back but understood pretty quickly he was wedged in too well. In other words, stuck. Adrenaline kicking into high gear, Luke settled into the space half inside the room and half out and leveled his weapon toward the hallway.

"Special Agent Campbell?"

Ice gripped Luke's chest and lowered his core temperature in the split second when he heard the voice. He knew instantly whom it belonged to. Rob.

Was he about to show his face? Finally reveal himself?

That would make Luke's job a helluva lot easier. "You're welcome to come in. I seriously doubt you'll like what you find in here."

A figure lurked just beside the door frame.

Luke took aim but couldn't get off a good round. If he could get a clean shot, he wouldn't hesitate to take it. If not, he wouldn't risk his bullet passing through Sheetrock and into an unintended target.

Rob's eardrum-piercing chuckle split the air.

"You think that's funny? Why not go man-to-man for a change instead of creeping around, preying on innocent women?"

"I doubt you'd understand." Rob's voice was high-pitched, agitated.

Had Luke hit a nerve? Think he cared? Think again.

If the monster showed himself, Luke was ready, which was exactly the reason he knew Rob wouldn't bite. He was an opportunist. Like a vulture, he waited until his prey was too vulnerable to fight back.

The barrel of a shotgun poked into the room.

If Luke repositioned now, could he get a better angle? "You want to kill me in cold blood?"

No answer.

"What? You can't talk all of a sudden? We both know that's not usually your problem, now, is it?" Just a little more to the left. Luke leaned, the window frame blocking his view. "Normally, you're a regular Chatty Cathy. And just as ignorant. Like your mother."

Luke was goading Rob on purpose, trying to see if he could throw him off his game. All Luke needed was one little slip. He was right there. So close Luke could hear the SOB breathe.

If he squeezed the trigger, moved his finger a fraction of an inch, Rob might just drop to the floor. But Luke was responsible for every bullet he discharged and he couldn't risk one going astray. There were too many innocent lives around and his bullet would easily pierce these walls.

"You think you can outsmart me, don't you, Special Agent Campbell?" The voice was somber. Depressed? Did Rob suffer from depression? "You don't understand anything about me or my family."

"No. I don't. Afraid I don't speak ignorant, either."

"I can assure you that your insults won't get you where you'd like to go." Rob's high-pitched chortle belied his words. The controlled anger in his tone said otherwise.

"Let me ask you something, *Rick*. Why not fight me? You know, one-on-one? Instead of always sneaking in the shadows. Hurting people who have done nothing to you." Luke paused, hoping for confirmation.

A choked laugh escaped. "That's where you're wrong. These women are far from innocent. And if I wanted to fight a man, I'd choose a more worthy adversary than you." Rick didn't deny the fact he was Rob.

The floor creaked in the hallway. Rick was on the move, heading the wrong direction.

Luke knew Rick was already gone but needed a visual to confirm. Of course, if he wedged himself back inside the bedroom that would give Rick time to get to Julie on the lawn.

Stuck in the pane, Luke couldn't move another inch, leaving Julie unprotected. Did Rick realize that, too?

"Keep your gun ready and shoot anyone who comes out that front door or around the side of the building, Julie." He hoped she heard him.

Luke patiently worked his way through the window, keeping one eye on the room and his hand secured around the butt of his Glock. He managed to squeeze through the opening and shimmy the rest of the way out the window.

He dropped to the ground, scanned the perimeter and motioned for Julie to follow him around the side of the building.

Her hand visibly shook, but to her credit, she held the gun and her composure intact. *That's my girl.*

On Luke's way to the front of the house, he made a call to his boss to provide an update. Backup was a block away. By the time he reached the streets, he knew in his gut that Rob was gone.

Frustration flooded him. Sirens wailed toward him as he conducted a thorough search of the perimeter just to be sure.

He gave a statement to the uniformed officer who arrived on the scene. The officer who'd been stationed on the street was confirmed dead.

With a heavy chest, Luke walked Julie to his truck.

"We have to move. Find another safe house. Or, better yet, just stay on the road."

Julie fastened her seat belt. "How can he be behind us every step? How can he anticipate our moves?"

"He's cunning."

If Rick knew where Luke lived, he'd also know what he drove. Then he remembered that Rick had been on their tail ever since they'd left the TV station. Everything snapped into place. His head pounded.

"Hold on." Luke popped out of the driver's seat.

"What is it, Luke?"

He examined the bottom of the truck again, running his hand along the boards. Nothing. He popped the hood next and checked every part. The filter. The engine. He ran his hand along the drivetrain and released a string of curse words. "Guy figured out what I was driving. He put a tracker on us."

"So he's been following our movements ever since the TV station?"

"Guess he figured he needed insurance in case you got away. We played right into his hands." Luke removed the device and palmed it. "Now the question is, what do we do with this?"

"Toss it?"

"Not unless I want him to know I found it. No. This is too valuable. And our first real break. He doesn't realize we've made the discovery." Luke tucked the small piece of metal in his front jeans' pocket.

"No, Luke. Turn it in. Get rid of it." Her body visibly shuddered. "Won't your boss know what to do with it? Maybe he can destroy it. Send it to the bottom of the Trinity River."

"Don't worry about it. I know exactly what to do." Luke had a plan. He'd lead the bastard away from her.

JULIE DIDN'T KNOW what Luke intended to do with that device, but she had a bad feeling he had no inclination to clue her in. Or was it just a bad feeling in general? Probably a little bit of both. Being close to a murderer moments ago had her skin crawling.

Then again, there wasn't much about this situation that she liked. Worse yet, he'd shut down again, cut her out. The gleam in his eyes said he had an idea. The determined set to his jaw said he didn't intend to share, either.

There was so much about him now that was different than before. She'd never felt closer to him in so many ways. And yet, even though her heart wanted to believe this was different, how could it be? Not if he continued to shut her out at critical times.

A feeling of stupidity washed over her.

Wasn't past behavior the best predictor of future actions? And yet, hadn't she clung to the slim hope this time would be different? That he'd changed?

Was that even possible?

Didn't she read somewhere that behavior was the hardest thing to change? Even if someone wanted to?

There were signs of his PTSD returning, too. The headaches. The sleepless nights. The night sweats.

At least he was talking this time, a little voice reminded her. Not completely shutting her out like before.

Yeah. She guessed that was true.

And yet, he wasn't opening up about what he planned to do with that device.

"Luke, talk to me. Please."

He maneuvered onto the on-ramp of Interstate 75. "Everything will be okay. We're making progress, Julie."

Adrenaline caused his hands to shake on the wheel.

Julie had sat by idly before, but she refused to do it now. If she'd learned one thing, it was that she had to fight for what she loved. "Don't shut me out, Luke. Don't you dare shut me out."

He must've realized the implication of what she said because he immediately exited the highway and parked in a retail lot. "I wouldn't do that to you, Julie."

"You are. I see what's going on, Luke. It's happening again."

"No. It's not. This is different. I need you to trust that I know what I'm doing." He held her gaze as he leaned toward her and captured her face in his hands. "I love you. Nothing is going to change that."

"Look what this is doing to you, Luke."

"I'll do whatever it takes to protect you. That much is

true. This case has been hell." The weariness in his eyes made her ache.

"I need to know you're not going to disappear on me again."

"You have my word."

If only she could be certain. "You know I love you."

"Then believe in me. This is different."

"How? You can't sleep. You're having nightmares again. What's different this time?"

"I know what's at stake. I have you to talk to. And I have been telling you as much as I can."

She couldn't deny he was including her for the most part. "But you're hiding something now."

She steadied herself for the lie.

"You're right."

If she hadn't been sitting, his admission would've knocked her off balance. "Then how is this different? Give me something to hang on to."

"I know what I'm doing now. I can't tell you everything, but as soon as this is over, I will. You have no idea how much I need you."

She held on to his gaze.

"But you can't tell me anything else?"

"Not yet. I need to know you have faith in me."

She answered with a kiss and a silent prayer he'd come back alive.

## Chapter Sixteen

Luke figured his best chance to draw Rick out was to use himself as bait. He'd drop Julie off with Detective Garcia and park himself somewhere. But where?

His first choice would be an open place like the Katy Trail. SWAT could easily hide in the nearby trees and cover the perimeter. Or if he used the Nature Preserve in Plano, then snipers could surround the parking lot. When Rick so much as stepped out of his vehicle, he'd be arrested or shot. Problem solved.

But that wasn't the case here. Rick would realize something was off in an instant. Luke would not take Julie to a park randomly in the middle of the day. A restaurant wouldn't work, either. Too public. Rick had already proved he'd kill innocent people if it meant gaining his freedom.

A motel? Nope. Where else? Luke navigated back onto the highway. "I need to investigate a lead."

"I already know the answer to this question, but I'm going to ask anyway. You mean by yourself?"

"Yes."

"And you don't plan to tell me where you're going or who you're investigating?"

"No."

"Is it too dangerous for me to come?"

"Yes." Was he closing himself off to her? He didn't

think so. The only reason he didn't tell her was he didn't want to compromise her.

Hold on.

Was that true?

Or was he falling down that hole again, taking on everything himself? Not allowing her to share in his pain? His hurt?

Keeping his emotions bottled up under the guise he was protecting her?

Luke took a deep breath and kept his focus on the road. "I plan to see if I can draw him out using the tracking device I found on the truck."

He prepared himself for the fallout, expecting her to protest that the mission was too dangerous.

"Where do you plan for all this to happen?"

"Haven't decided that part yet."

He didn't need to look at her to know she was assessing him. She studied him for a long moment.

"What about that ranch in McKinney? It's isolated enough to keep people safe, but other officers could hide in the brush." There was no anger in her voice. Concern and caring were the only notes he detected.

"That was my next thought, too." Luke needed to quit underestimating her. She'd proved she could handle just about anything thrown her way. It was time he acknowledged it. "Grab the phone out of my pocket and dial Detective Garcia's number."

She did.

"Place the call on speaker."

Garcia answered on the second ring.

Luke identified himself. "You're on speaker, Detective. Julie Davis is on the line, as well. I need a favor."

"Name it. This have anything to do with our serial killer?"

"He's my only concern right now. I need more people and a personal guarantee."

"Done."

Luke filled the detective in on the plan to draw out Rick and the location. "One more thing. I want to keep Jul— the victim—out of sight. Here's where the personal guarantee comes into play. You're the only one I trust to keep her safe until I get back."

"I won't take my eyes off her, man."

"Appreciate it."

"Where should we meet?"

"Knox and Henderson." He'd feel a lot safer if she were in Dallas, far away, when he trapped Rick in McKinney.

"Will do. See you in ten minutes."

Julie ended the call and sat quietly on the ride to the meeting point. They beat Garcia, so Luke parked and waited.

He wished he knew what she was thinking. "Scared?"

"For you."

"Don't be. This is my job. Believe it or not, I'm pretty good at it." He cracked a smile, trying to ease the tension.

"I know. It's just…"

"What?"

"I don't want to lose you again." A few tears fell.

"You won't. Besides, I'm not the one he wants."

"He's already killed two officers who got in his way."

She had a point. He could sugarcoat this all day, but that wasn't exactly being fair to her. "Look. There are dangers to my job. Not just this case. This is what I do, who I am, and I need to know you can handle it."

"I did all right before…" She blew out a breath. "It's you I'm worried about."

He resisted the urge to curse. She was right. She hadn't tried to stop him from doing his job. This was who he was.

He was the one who'd come home and proved he couldn't handle it. She'd been more than willing to stick around and help him through what he was experiencing.

He captured her hand in his and brought her fingers to his lips, kissing the tips of each one. Promises sat heavy. He wanted to be able to tell her everything would be okay, but she deserved proof. "You're right."

This wasn't the time for talk. He needed to show her that he could come back from anything life threw at them and still be himself. How did he tell her there wasn't anything Rick or anyone else could do to him personally that would affect him? The only thing that could hurt him was if Rick got to her.

He unhooked her seat belt and pulled her next to him. "I'm stronger because of you."

Julie looked him straight in the eye. "You come back to me in one piece as soon as this is done."

"You have my word." And he meant it.

He kissed her, hard. Needing to remember the way she tasted, just in case things didn't go as planned.

Detective Garcia pulled alongside them.

"Be safe," Julie said before switching cars.

"Keep a close eye on her for me," he said to Garcia.

"Won't let her out of my sight."

"Thank you." They exchanged a few details about the meet-up location and where Garcia planned to take her. "Call me if anything changes. And if—"

"You just worry about keeping metal out of your own butt," Garcia said. "I'll protect her."

Luke nodded his thanks, put the truck in Drive and navigated out of the lot.

A half hour later, he parked at the McKinney safe house. It sat on an acre of land in northern Collin County. The location was perfect. It'd be impossible for anyone to drive up or get close with a vehicle unnoticed. ATVs and motorcycles were too noisy to use.

Normally, ops took weeks to plan where intel was gathered and scenarios ran through dozens of times before executing. But a small window of opportunity existed here. Luke had no plans to waste any possible advantage he could squeeze out of this.

The house was considered as part of a suburb but the neighbors were far enough away to keep them out of danger. Before Luke arrived, he'd picked up enough supplies to last the night. The place had a male quality to the decor, meaning there wasn't much furniture except what was absolutely necessary. A slipcovered couch and a TV tray for an end table were in the living room. The small dining nook had a table with four chairs. They all matched but looked like relics from the seventies. Especially the wallpaper in the kitchen. Those hues of green and yellow had seen better days.

There was no TV. Today, the place would've been described as open-concept living, dining, kitchen with one bedroom off the living room, but Luke suspected when it was built, the place would've been described as quaint.

If Luke put a kitchen chair in the middle of the open-concept space and opened the door to the bedroom and bathroom, he could see every possible entry point into the place.

He moved to the bedroom and, using the key he'd been given when he used the place last month, unlocked the safe. He pulled an AR-15 and loaded a magazine of silver-tip bullets into the clip. He closed the door, slid the key into his back pocket and pulled a chair into the middle of the room.

Even though he couldn't see any of the SWAT officers, he knew they were there, watching. If something happened to Luke, they still had more than a good chance of capturing Rick. Either way, Julie would be safe.

Of course, Luke's plan involved capturing the bad guy and returning in good health to spend a considerable amount of time with the woman he loved. Preferably naked. If he had anything to say about it, spending the rest of his life with Julie would be a good place to start.

Now all he had to do was sit and wait.

JULIE CLICKED OFF her seat belt and followed Detective Garcia into the small ranch-style house.

"I'd like you to meet my wife, Pilar." The woman he referred to was a couple of inches shorter than Julie and had shoulder-length straight brown hair. Her almond-shaped brown eyes were mirrored in the child's, balanced on her hip. She turned from the stove and smiled. "Welcome to our home."

"Thank you for having me." Julie was corralled to the dinner table along with Garcia.

They were joined by a child who couldn't have been more than five years old.

"This is my son, Juan Jr. Pilar is holding our daughter, Maria."

"You have a beautiful family, Detective."

Pilar set a plate of enchiladas on the table, followed by a bowl of soup. "I hope you like authentic Mexican food."

"Love," Julie said with a smile. What time was it? Luke had to be there by now. Was he okay? Was Rick there, too?

When everyone had a plate, the little one clasped his hands together and pinched his eyes shut. *"Padre—"*

"In English for our guest," Garcia said.

Julie's heart squeezed for how adorable the little boy was as he blushed.

"Sorry, missus."

"No. It's beautiful the way you say it. Go ahead."

"Bless us, oh Lord—" he sighed before continuing "—in these gifts we receive from you. A-men."

"Amen," Julie echoed, ignoring the pain in her chest. For the rest of the meal, she vacillated between wanting Luke's plan to work and wanting it to fail. Either way, she feared for Luke's life.

Even though the food smelled amazing, she couldn't imagine being able to eat. She didn't want to be rude, so she managed to get enough bites down that she wouldn't offend the Garcias' generosity.

Seeing the sweet family gathered around the dinner table made her heart ache to have her own family someday.

There was a time—not so long ago—when she'd thought she and Luke would be holding their own child by now. The image of Hitch's angelic face stamped her thoughts.

Would their baby look anything like its adorable cousin?

Would they ever get the chance to find out?

Instead of dreaming of their future, they were running for their lives from a determined serial killer.

Not running. Not anymore. Luke had placed himself directly in Rick's sights in order to draw him away from her.

She couldn't imagine a future without Luke.

Reality hit hard.

Life could change in a heartbeat. An instant—a changed appointment—was all it had taken to alter her course forever. And yet, it had brought her back to Luke.

Was that destiny?

Would it be his to die at the hands of a monster after surviving so much?

Julie refocused. She had to think positive thoughts for Luke. Nothing could happen to the man she loved. Not again.

She didn't look at the detective when she asked, "Have you heard anything?"

"Not yet." He waited until she met his eyes. "But we will."

With everything inside her, she prayed he was right.

## Chapter Seventeen

Four hours and sixteen minutes into the mission, Luke started thinking this had been a bad idea. He'd received a coded text message from Garcia letting him know everything was okay. No matter how much he trusted the detective, his first choice would have been to take Julie to the ranch and have his brothers, Nick and Reed, watch over her.

There simply hadn't been time. Considering they'd pieced this mission together in a matter of an hour, everything had fallen into place well. Even so, not having his own eyes on Julie left him feeling unsettled and tense.

The small ranch mostly used for training exercises made for a perfect location. Four SWAT officers were positioned outside on the grounds in various locations.

Luke sat squarely in the center of the place for so long, his legs were going numb. He stood, dropped to the ground and did twenty push-ups to get the blood flowing again. To his backside was a solid wall. No chance Rick could surprise Luke with this setup.

A dull thump pounded between his ears as a flashback rocked him. This was different, he reminded himself as he rubbed his eyes.

Luke shook off the memory. He was no longer alone. He had Julie.

Movement to his left caught his attention. A shadow crossed the window. House lights were on outside, making it brighter than inside, affording a better view. He had company.

Luke readjusted his earpiece and alerted the SWAT team that they had a guest outside the building. He raised his AR-15 to his shoulder and aimed the scope toward the front door.

His eyes had long adjusted to the darkness. He relied on his other senses, too. A noise came in the direction of the bathroom. If this was Rick, he was not in the house yet.

Luke repositioned his scope, lining his crosshairs with the center of the shower door. Adrenaline pulsed through him in audible waves. Every sense heightened, on fight alert.

He changed position, crouching next to the sofa, and then relayed his new position to SWAT. Rick set foot inside this house and this whole ordeal would be all over.

Another noise came from the other side of the house this time. Luke reached for his thermal binoculars. They confirmed SWAT's presence, but where was Rick?

Luke didn't so much as breathe as he listened for anything that would give him a position on Rick. Find that bastard in the crosshairs of his scope and Luke wouldn't think twice about doing what needed to be done, especially considering how dangerous the man was.

But there was nothing.

Luke cursed under his breath and then relayed the message to SWAT. Everything had been quiet for ten minutes. Instinct said Rick was gone. Could they get to him before he got too far away?

"This party has moved on. I'm going hunting." Luke wasn't about to give up until he knew for certain the search was over.

Ringtones sounded. Luke palmed his cell and checked caller ID. His boss. "What's the word?"

"There's been another murder."

"Him?"

"We believe so. It has his signature written all over it."

"Where?" In the hours he'd waited for Rick, could he have been saving someone's life? Luke took down the address, ended the call and loaded his GPS.

He bit back a curse.

While he'd been waiting for Rick, taking up valuable resources, the SOB had killed someone right down the street. Anger and frustration engulfed him, lighting a fire that had been simmering since Iraq. Another person was dead because of Luke's misjudgment.

The familiar sting of shame pierced him, spreading throughout his body like a flesh-eating bacteria. There was no one to blame but Luke. He'd been shortsighted, acted too quickly, and Rick had capitalized on the mistake.

Luke drove the couple of blocks to the scene. A squad car, lights blazing, was parked in front of the house. A uniformed officer stood on the front lawn of the small ranch house, taking a statement from, most likely, a neighbor.

Luke fished for his gloves in the console and pulled them on.

Eating up the real estate in a few short strides, he flashed his badge and made a beeline for the front door.

The kill had to be fresh because there was no stench coming from the house as he crossed the threshold.

Inside, the scene played out the same way the others had. A black-haired woman, decapitated, sprawled across the couch. Her arms folded, her legs crossed. Luke fisted his hands, angry with himself for allowing the monster to strike again. Did he blame himself? Yeah.

Did he take it personally? Hell yes.

It was his responsibility to catch this creep and get him off the streets. Every time he was allowed to breathe air freely and strike again, Luke failed.

There'd been an attempt to clean up the blood, but splatter marks were everywhere. A substance that looked and smelled a lot like bleach soaked her clothes. Nothing else in the place had been touched.

The house was clean, so there were no dust tracks to indicate if anything had been removed. The place was small but neatly kept.

A few personal pictures of the woman and a child at various stages of the child's life were neatly placed around the room.

The whole scene smacked of Rick.

Guilt ate at Luke's insides. If he'd chosen a different neighborhood, this woman would still be alive. Her child would not suffer the horror she was about to face. Life would go on normally for the two of them.

He'd just cost a child her mother. He swore under his breath. His fingers fisted and released.

Was he beating himself up over this mentally? Yeah. Losing another life to this monster was something Luke would always take personally.

He had to remind himself to calm down. Maintaining his cool could mean the difference between being too hasty and missing something important that might lead to finding the life-stealing jerk who was responsible.

Luke walked the house, checking every window, picture and piece of furniture for clues. He'd check and double-check everything just in case.

The officer who'd been interviewing witnesses stepped inside the house and called for Luke. He met the man in uniform in the hall.

"Did the neighbors see anything?" Luke asked.

"No, sir. I canvassed the surrounding houses after securing the area. No one saw anything out of the ordinary."

"No sudden noises? Screaming?"

He shook his head.

"What's her name?"

"Kimberly Jackson, sir."

"Thank you. Has her next of kin been notified?" Luke opened the notebook app on his phone.

"No, sir. Not yet."

"You have kids?"

"A two-year-old and a newborn."

"Must keep you busy."

"Can't remember what it's like to sleep for more than six hours at a stretch," the officer said, easing his stance.

"Ms. Jackson has a daughter. There doesn't seem to be a father. Can you do me a favor and see to it that her daughter doesn't see her like this? No little girl should have to see her mother in this condition."

"I hear you, sir. Will do. I can't even imagine anything like this happening to my wife."

Luke nodded agreement. "Any idea how the guy got inside?"

"Didn't see any signs of forced entry."

How had Rick charmed his way inside? The likelihood he'd planned this out in advance was slim. This was a crime of opportunity.

"Thanks a lot. For everything," Luke said. Another question ate at him. Why? What good would it do to kill someone here? This was outside his usual kill zone.

The logical answer nearly buckled Luke's knees. Rick already knew where he believed Luke and Julie were, based on the tracking device, and he wanted to create a distraction. Had he hoped to create enough of a diversion to snatch Julie from the scene?

How had he gained entry when nothing indicated the use of force?

Luke scanned the area.

A fresh bouquet of flowers sat in the middle of the kitchen island. A weight lodged itself inside the pit of Luke's stomach as he moved toward the yellow roses.

There was a card. He pulled a small evidence bag from his back jeans' pocket, then opened the note.

It read "She has to pay."

Rick had figured them out. He knew.

The diversion wasn't created to snatch Julie from here. Luke released a string of swearwords. The air sucked out of his lungs in a whoosh at the same time his cell phone sounded, because he already knew Rick wasn't talking about the woman in the next room. He palmed his phone and studied the screen, barely aware he was already in a dead run toward his truck. The text from his boss read...

Garcia's missing.

JULIE FOUGHT THE darkness surrounding her, draining her. A blow to the back of her head had left her nauseated and with a pounding headache, but she forced herself to stay awake and remember what had happened.

Her brain was mush, but a picture began to emerge. The detective had been called into the station. She and Garcia had been walking toward his car when they'd been ambushed. The last thing she remembered was the detective grabbing his chest after a shot had been fired. *Garcia*.

Julie said a silent prayer he would be okay. She couldn't imagine having to look into the eyes of his beautiful children or wife and tell them he was no longer coming through that door or sitting at their dinner table.

Pain so overwhelming and powerful it was like a physical punch assaulted her. Where was Luke?

What had happened to him? Had Rick gotten to him before he'd attacked them?

Another stab of pain tightened her gut at the memory of being thrown in the trunk of a gray Volkswagen Jetta. Looking into Rick's dead black eyes would haunt her for the rest of her life. Which might not be all that much longer if she didn't figure a way out of this car.

Didn't all trunks have an emergency-release lever?

It was hard to move with her hands bound behind her back. Her ankles had been tied together with rope. Could she wiggle enough to break free?

Rick must've been a Boy Scout, because, try as she might, she couldn't gain an inch.

There was only one of him. As much as he seemed superhuman, he was only a man. Men had weaknesses. She would find Rick's and fight him to the death. His intentions were clear. Her throat dried up just thinking about what he'd done to her client, what he would do to her.

Maybe Rick had been in such a hurry, he'd allowed Garcia a chance to live.

Julie bounced around in the trunk. A speed bump? She listened for any sounds that might help her figure out where he was taking her or give her an edge when describing her location later.

No situation was hopeless, she repeated to herself quietly as tears spilled out of her eyes. There had to be a way to escape.

Sirens blared past her. She was still in the city.

How long had they been in the car?

She'd panicked at first. It took her a little while to get her bearings. How much time had she lost in the interim? Ten minutes? Twenty?

Foreboding numbed her limbs. She had to fight it. This couldn't be over yet. Julie worked the restraints on her wrists again. She couldn't get any traction there. She kicked her feet and screamed.

"Be quiet back there." The voice was almost a nervous squeal. Freaked out?

He should be.

Julie had no plans to go down without a fight. What was the worst that could happen? She knew what he had planned and couldn't think of a more hateful way to kill someone.

Trying to reason with this guy wouldn't do any good, either.

Fear barked at her, threatening to consume her. She refused to allow it. If she allowed terror to paralyze her, he'd already won. His victims must've been scared to death in their final moments.

He could do what he wanted with her body, and probably would, but he couldn't touch her mind. She alone had the power to control her thoughts. And she refused to give him the satisfaction of knowing she was afraid.

The car came to a stop before he cut the engine.

This was it.

Julie positioned herself on her back and bent her knees.

The trunk opened and she released a scream, thrusting her feet toward Rick's face.

His head knocked back. He swore, grabbing at his nose and checking for blood. Before he could grab her, she kicked again. Hard. With all the fear and anger she had balled inside her.

He stumbled back while cursing her then disappeared. "Be still. Wouldn't want to have to knock you out before I kill you."

Julie expected to be out in the country, far from the city. But she could hear cars. A highway?

All she could see were stars against the curtain of a black sky. There was a brisk chill in the air.

She curled her legs, ready to strike again.

This time, he surprised her from the side. A quick blow to the head and she struggled to remain conscious. "He won't let you get away with this. You hurt me and he won't stop until he finds you."

She was baiting him, but she hoped he'd tell her what he'd done with Luke. Because if her FBI agent was alive, she doubted she'd be in the back of a trunk, fighting for her life right now.

The thought of anything happening to Luke made it hard to breathe.

Another blow to the head and she wouldn't have to worry about it. She remembered Luke trying to make him angry to force a mistake. Could she do the same?

Her heart hammered against her ribs. The simple act of taking in air hurt.

Let her panic control her, and she'd be dead for sure.

What if Luke lay in a ditch somewhere? What if she could help?

She had to try.

"Come back, jerk, and give me a fair fight."

"I should have taped your mouth shut is what I should've done." His tone was frantic, almost hysterical.

"What's the matter? Don't like being rushed?"

A siren wailed in the distance.

"They're coming for you, Rick."

No reaction.

"How about I call you a simpleminded jerk instead? That is what you are. You think you're clever but you're not." She listened for a long moment.

Nothing.

"You're nothing more than a leech, sucking the blood out of innocent people."

"That's where you're wrong. They're filthy. People are dirty. Mother always said women are nasty creatures who will hurt you the way she hurt me. She was preparing me for my life as an adult. But she has to pay for her sins, too."

She tracked the voice to her left, repositioning her feet in order to deliver a crushing blow as soon as those blue eyes appeared. "Your mom sounds as insane as you."

"Ask your FBI agent how stupid I am. Oh, right, you can't. He's dead."

The blow from those words knocked the wind out of her. Was it true? Her heart screamed no. Rick would say anything to throw her off balance. Exactly what she was doing to him. "Might be. But you won't get away with this. They know who you are. You go home and they've got you. They know your family. There's nowhere left to hide."

A hysterical laugh came from the right.

Julie quickly adjusted her positioning.

"Impossible."

"Is that so? How can you be so sure?"

"I would've seen it on the news."

"Like they'd tell those jerks." Her best bet was to stall for time.

Silence.

"What's the matter? Didn't figure that part out already? They swarmed your house. Found everything. One of the officers called you a deviant."

"You're lying." His tone sounded agitated now. "I'm the most sane person they'll ever meet. Besides, I can tell you're making it up. People wouldn't say that about me. I'm too smart and they know it. Smarter than your FBI boyfriend, that's for sure."

He'd moved closer on the right side.

She repositioned, remembering something Luke had told her about serial killers. "Sorry to tell you, bud, they know who you are. Leave here and you'll spend the rest of your life as a scrawny girlfriend to a man named T-Bone in prison. Guess what? T-Bone won't like the fact you make wigs from your victims' hair. People who kill innocent women rank right up there with pedophiles in prison."

He rose up from the side of the car, anger radiating from his slender frame.

Julie kicked with everything she had inside her.

Rick sidestepped in time to avoid the thrust of her foot. She made a move to reposition, but before she could fire off another blow, her legs were captured. She tried to break free, but even with the extra strength another shot of adrenaline provided, the grip around her ankles was too strong.

A quick smirk followed by an even faster blow to the head stunned Julie as her vision blurred.

Before she could get her bearings, she was on the ground being dragged. Every movement hurt. She raised her head to stop it from being scraped along the pavement, screaming, fighting with everything she had inside her.

"You shouldn't talk to me like that, Mother. All I ever wanted was your approval," Rick mumbled. "You've been bad, too. You have to tell me you love me. You'll do that once I cleanse you. Won't you, Mother?"

What was he talking about? She glanced around. And who was he talking to?

Julie bucked and wiggled, still screaming, but his grasp was too tight. He hauled her in front of a storage unit as if she weighed nothing. He unlocked and opened the door using one hand.

Light streamed inside as Rick shoved her against the wall, forcing her to sit up. All she could see in front of her were boxes. "Please, don't go through with this. Let me go."

Rick moved to the center of the room, his body blocking her view.

He turned around. She got a glimpse of what he held in his hands and her heart pitched. In his grasp, he held a half-made wig of black hair.

Bile burned the back of her throat. She screamed as he forced her to be still, placing the wig on top of her head.

"Be still, Mother. You mustn't get upset with me." He withdrew. A hurt look crossed his features. "Bad things happen when you get angry."

"I'm not her. I'm not your mother. Let me go."

"All I ever wanted was for you to love me, Mother. As usual, you deny me." He rose up, fury rising with him. "Why won't you love me?"

He struck Julie again.

Then everything went black.

# *Chapter Eighteen*

Luke had hit Redial for the tenth time in a row when his cell buzzed. He answered his boss's call immediately.

"We found Detective Garcia a block from his house." His solemn tone sent a fireball of dread rocketing through Luke's stomach.

"Alive?"

"Yes. He took a beating, but he's on his way to Parkland Memorial. The EMT said he's in bad shape, but his numbers are strong."

"And the woman who was with him?" Luke steeled his resolve, fighting against the overwhelming urge to slam his fist into something. Anything.

The beat of silence his boss gave him wasn't a good sign. "I'm sorry, Luke. He got her and disappeared."

A torpedo couldn't have pierced his heart more deeply. "Any witnesses? Any idea where he took her?"

"We have a guy who's talking. He saw a man force a woman into a gray Volkswagen Jetta and head east. We have men combing the area. A chopper's already in the air."

Luke fisted his free hand. "Who else is on the investigation?"

"I have all my men on the case. Rogers, Stevens, Segal. Everyone. Dallas P.D. put some more power behind it.

We're canvassing Garcia's neighborhood, just in case someone saw something but is scared to come forward. I sent out an alert in the system. Plano, Richardson and Garland have teams ready to mobilize on a moment's notice. The BOLO's already out. I got every bit of my people available working toward finding her."

Given enough time, his boss's words would be comforting. The names he'd mentioned would put the pieces together and produce a location. The sand had drained from the hourglass, and Luke had no time to wait.

"You know I appreciate everything you're doing."

"Goes without saying. We're checking property records, the DMV. If this guy or any of his family members own so much as an RV, we'll be on it."

"Thanks for the update. If I get any leads on my end, I'll keep you posted." He needed to end the call. Right now, he wanted—no, needed—to punch something, and he didn't want to risk being pulled from the case for going ballistic.

How could he not?

It was Julie.

His boss knew about the personal connection, and Luke had half expected to be yanked. Figured he hadn't been because he'd been able to put up a good front. He was human. No doubt every agent would feel the same way if one of their loved ones was in a similar situation. The boss would, too. He sure wouldn't sit in an ivory tower and hope for the best. He'd be out beating the pavement with the rest of them.

Luke needed to refocus and recap what he knew about Rick. The guy was sneaky. Luke had to give him that. Bright. The guy liked a good diversion. While they'd been trying to lure him into a trap, Rick had murdered a woman and then got to Garcia. The noises at the ranch couldn't have been him.

Why would he risk killing so close to Luke?

Obviously, to kill again. He seemed to enjoy operating on the edge of being caught. Could that mean he wouldn't take Julie far?

Luke's cell buzzed. Nick's name came up on the screen. "What do you have for me?"

"Reed's also on the line. I put the call on conference. What do you know so far?"

He recounted the day's events.

"Man, I'm sorry. I know how much she means to you," Nick said.

"I'm already digging around in the backgrounds of everyone connected to Rick Camden, financial records," Reed chimed in.

"Your support means the world."

"Reed's contacts through Border Patrol can move mountains," Nick said.

"We'll know something in the next few minutes," Reed said. He paused a beat. "Hold on. I have news. Guess what? His dad rents a storage unit at the crossroads of George Bush and Preston. It's a Dallas address. On the southwest side."

Luke bolted toward his truck. "I know that location. I've driven past it a thousand times. It's just off the street. The place is blocked because of the highway."

"Be careful, bro. We'll send Riley for backup. He shouldn't be too far since you'll be at Plano's back door," Nick said.

Luke tossed the cell on the passenger seat as he turned over the ignition, praying he wouldn't be too late. He couldn't lose Julie again. Not like this.

His only real question was whether or not he'd get there in time to make a difference. Flashbacks of the night he lost his men in Iraq assaulted him as he navigated through the evening traffic in frigid temperatures.

That same helpless, angry feeling enveloped him now as he neared the storage facility.

He gunned the engine and weaved through cars and trucks.

The intersection was busy, but, just as he remembered, the facility was off the road, hidden by the wall that was built to block noise from George Bush Highway onto a nearby neighborhood.

Using hands-free, he called his boss to let him know he'd arrived. He left clear instructions with everyone to creep in. No lights. No sirens.

He ended the call letting his boss know he had no plans to wait for backup.

The gate was closed and this facility did not have on-site personnel. He knew that from past experience dealing with the owners. Security would be loose. An iron fence enclosed the place and there were cameras positioned in the corners. These conditions were perfect for a man like Rick. Man? No. Animal.

A real man wouldn't hurt women.

Luke strapped his AR-15 to his back and scaled the metal fence in one giant hop. A security gate wouldn't keep him from taking down this monster. Without sirens, he had no idea how close backup was, so he wasn't alarmed by the fact he heard none. But it wouldn't be far away.

Either way, he couldn't afford to hang around and wait.

THE PLACE WAS COLD, dark and eerily quiet. Julie worked her hands behind her back, trying to loosen the rope. She hadn't managed any progress so far. After the last time she'd screamed, a piece of tape had been placed over her mouth.

Had someone heard her? Stopped him?

No. If they had, wouldn't she be safe right now instead

of locked in a storage room, wearing a wig the sicko had made from his victims?

Tears slid down her cheeks as fear gripped her. Detective Garcia was most likely dead. She couldn't begin to think about his sweet family when they heard the news. Whatever Rob had done to Garcia, his plans for her would be much more sinister.

Where had he gone? Worse yet, when would he be back?

He'd secured her and disappeared. Painfully aware he could return at any time, she pressed her back against the wall and tried to push up.

She struggled against her bindings. Fear caused her hands to shake, making it that much more difficult to work the knot. Damn that she couldn't break free. If she could surprise him, she might have a chance.

A little piece of her prayed Luke would find her. But what if he was…? No. She couldn't allow herself to think like that. Lose hope and it might as well all be over.

The wind howled, her heart pounding faster with every gust. Could she work the knot? Her fingers fumbled around for the bow in the rope. No use. Her eyes were beginning to adjust to the darkness. Was there anything she could use? She squinted, trying to make out shapes, but couldn't get a clear look.

Could she scoot to the door and wiggle out before he got back? Surely there were security cameras. Wouldn't someone be watching? Only one thing was certain. Sit there. Do nothing. And she was already dead.

The bindings around her ankles made it difficult to scoot across the floor. She rocked her body until she inched forward.

A gust of wind slammed against the metal door. She couldn't suppress a yelp.

There were more noises, which sounded like feet shuffling.

Couldn't be wind this time. Rick was back.

Her heart hammered her ribs as she tensed her body and clenched her fists, preparing for whatever walked under the metal sliding door.

She worked her jaw from side to side, trying to loosen the tape because as soon as that metal grate lifted, she planned to scream.

Was there anything else around she could use? She scanned the enclosure but could see only general shapes and nothing specific.

If she could scoot a little closer to the door, she could bang her head against it and make a loud noise. Anyone around would hear it. Except she was reasonably certain there was no one else around but her and Rick.

Julie managed to inch closer to the door. She held her breath, half expecting it to shoot up any moment and Rick to be standing there, that satisfied and haunting smirk on his face. With his blond hair, blue eyes and runner's build, she could see why he was disarming to women. He looked like a Boy Scout, not a murderer. Ravishing Rob. *Captivates then decapitates.* A chill gripped her, numbing her limbs.

Was that a pair of crutches leaning against the wall? Yet another in one of his many traps to disarm his prey? Blood ran cold in her veins.

How could someone be so cruel?

Movement outside the door gave her the ominous premonition that she was about to be next. Hesitating, waiting for a sign—any sign—that the person on the other side of that door wasn't Rick, she held her breath and listened. If she could manage to get a little closer, six more inches, she could make some noise. Maybe she could draw their attention. The footsteps came closer, paused, then moved on. Couldn't be him. Could it?

She banged her shoulder against the metal door, causing ripples of sound to roll through the room and the door to shake.

"Julie?" came out in a whisper, but the voice was unmistakable. Luke.

With the tape covering her mouth, she couldn't speak, but she didn't let that stop her from trying. She banged against the door again, with more force this time, and shouted—which came out like a muffled scream.

The door slid open enough for her to get a glimpse of him. Her body went limp from relief at seeing his face. Luke was alive. A flood of emotions descended on her like a hundred-foot wall of water.

He pulled the wig off, dropped to his knees and captured her face in his hands, his own emotion visible in the worry lines bracketing his mouth. He pulled the tape off her mouth. "I thought I'd lost—"

"Luke. He said you were gone." Her own emotions made her eyes fill with tears. "How did you find me?"

"My brothers tracked down this storage unit." His kiss was a mix of sweet and needy.

Her sense of relief and joy was short-lived as he immediately pulled back and surveyed the area. Luke's guard was up as he scanned the room. Enough light streamed in to see clearly.

"Where is he?" Luke asked.

"I don't know. He threw me in here and disappeared. I was screaming. Hoped someone heard me and interrupted him."

"He had to know the area was hot. Most likely plans to return later and finish the job. Even if he was caught, he'd still have his final revenge if no one found you." Luke turned to face the opening, his back against the wall as he pulled a knife from his pocket and cut the ropes. His gaze continued to sweep the area as he worked.

As soon as her hands were free, she rubbed them together, trying to bring feeling back.

"Let's get you out of here." Luke shifted his position quickly, and before she realized what he was doing, he'd cut the rope on her ankles, too. His handgun was leveled and ready to fire.

The blood rushed to her feet. She made a move to get up but landed on her backside.

"Give it a minute. Feeling will come back," Luke whispered.

The light streaming in from the door gave Julie a little perspective about what the storage facility was used for. She'd already seen the crutches, but there were other props. A wheelchair was in one corner. There was an open box filled with various ropes and handcuffs. There were tools like saws lying around. Boxes of garbage bags sat on the floor. Uniforms ranging from scrubs to local police blues were strewn around. He had everything he needed right there to get inside someone's house without using force.

Back where she sat, he'd spread several blankets on the floor. He must've been in too big of a hurry to tie her to the pole he'd installed.

Julie rubbed her hands together faster. She didn't want to be caught off guard if he returned. And he would come back. She needed to get the heck out of there.

Luke finished sweeping the area. "I can carry you, but that would leave us vulnerable. Can you walk?"

"I will." Julie pushed herself up and took a tentative step forward. "He's just going to let us walk out of here?"

"He doesn't get to decide." He handed her a weapon and shouldered his AR-15. "On my word, shoot. Got it?"

She nodded.

Squeezing her hand around the butt of the gun brought more feeling back. She followed closely as Luke led the way toward an iron fence to what she hoped would be freedom. Faint sounds of traffic from a freeway could be heard. If only she could move faster. As it was, adrenaline was the only thing keeping her upright.

She didn't recognize anything, but that was because Rick had covered her eyes before. With the parking lot in view, she lowered her weapon.

A blow came from behind, striking Julie on the crown of her head.

# *Chapter Nineteen*

"Luke!" Julie's scream wrapped around his spine like an ice pack.

He pivoted and leveled his weapon at Rick. With the SOB using Julie as a shield, Luke couldn't get a clean shot. She'd dropped her weapon and Rick had kicked it out of reach. The blade of a knife was pressed against her throat. Luke forced himself not to focus on the panicked look in her eyes.

"She doesn't get to live." Rick's agitated pitch was a far cry from his normal controlled tone. His voice practically shook from hysteria. The guy must not have wanted to risk being too far away in case she tried to escape.

"This is between us, Rick. Let her go."

"No. I need her. She's part of this, of me. You wouldn't understand."

Julie's body shuddered.

"She didn't do anything to hurt you. She's not your mother. Just another innocent woman." Luke walked a mental tightrope, balancing between angering and disarming Rick.

"We both know that's not true. She's your wife. I should slice her throat just for that." Rick turned his attention to her. "Don't worry. I'll be quick this time."

Luke needed to get the guy to focus on him. "I understand now. What your mom must've done to you. She made you angry, didn't she?"

Rick's laugh came out as a chortle. "I wouldn't push me if I were you. I can end it all now."

"Then tell me. Why do you hurt people weaker than you? That makes you just like her." He needed to keep Rick's attention away from Julie.

She gripped the arm braced against her chest with both hands. The knife was pressed so hard against her throat, Luke could see an indentation from it. A trickle of blood rolled down the blade. If Luke could somehow signal her to bite or fight, maybe he could get a clean shot. With that knife so close to her throat, even an accidental slip could cut her jugular vein. She'd bleed out before the ambulance arrived.

Luke inched forward, closing the five-foot gap between them a little more. If he could get close enough, maybe he could grab the knife or knock him off balance. Backup should arrive any minute.

Rick took two steps back. "Stay right where you are. Don't come any closer."

"You slit her throat and you've got nothing. I'll shoot you right here and now. And that's a promise."

Rick didn't move.

"What happened? With your mother?"

"She can't cut me out."

"What did she say?"

"That I was out of the family. She kicked me out of the house, just like that. Two years ago. After everything we'd been through. Said she was done with me."

"Why would she do that?"

"I told her I didn't want to play her sexual games anymore. I wanted a real girlfriend like my brother Chad had. And she cut me out of the family."

Luke looked at Julie, needing her to stay focused. He

angled his head back ever so slightly. Did she catch it? Did she understand what he was telling her to do?

She blinked her eyes several times quickly but didn't dare budge.

Good. She understood his message.

In the background, Luke heard several cars pull into the parking lot. The footsteps of what had to be several officers rushing toward them echoed across the empty space between the storage buildings.

"Make them go away. I'll kill us both." Rick was panicking. His gaze darted around and his face muscles pulled taut.

Luke instantly knew what Rick meant. He'd slice her throat and then make a move for an officer, forcing him to shoot. He didn't turn when he shouted, "Stay back!"

The footfalls stopped.

Rick wore the expression of a caged animal. He knew he was surrounded. No matter what else happened, the SOB wouldn't get away this time. There would be comfort in that thought if it didn't involve Julie. Blood trickled down her neck.

Except that none of this was good for Julie. And there was precious little Luke would be able to do to save her.

No way could he allow that to happen. He had to keep the officers back, as well. Maybe he could soften the guy. Make him think Luke was on his side. "There's another ending to this story, Rick. All three of us can walk out of here." He didn't add that one of them would be in handcuffs, but it was true.

"That's not how I see it going down." The lean man's hand shook. More trickles of Julie's blood ran down the blade.

"It doesn't have to be like this. You need help. I can arrange it for you."

Rick backed away a few more steps. If he managed another ten feet, he could slice her throat and disappear around the corner. And he would. Rick knew that Luke wouldn't let Julie die alone. His best chance of escape involved ensuring the woman Luke loved was dying.

"Make the officers go away, or she dies right here."

Luke bit back a curse. "Stay back or he'll do it. I'll meet you guys in the parking lot."

Rick took another step back. One more and it would be too late for Julie.

A distraction was needed. But what?

She must've sensed what was coming because she took a breath and then dropped down, buckling her knees. Her movement must've caught Rick off guard, because he fumbled for her, dropping the knife.

Luke lunged, wedging himself between Rick and Julie. At that moment, Rick punched her, knocking the wind out of her. Her weak ankles were unable to hold her weight, so she went down fast—a crack sounded, skull to pavement.

Luke fended off a potshot from Rick as he glanced down at her. "Julie."

Slumped on her side, she didn't answer.

Rick threw a punch that Luke blocked. He was stronger than the other man, but adrenaline did funny things to baseline strength. Not to mention the fact that Rick had everything to lose if he got caught.

A knife thrust at him. Luke ducked in time to miss the blade. He pivoted left and crouched low, getting a quick visual on Julie.

Her chest moved, so it meant she was breathing. *Hold on, sweetheart.*

Luke looked up in time to see an object the size of a coffee can being hurled at him. He deflected it with his forearm. What the hell was the jar filled with? Lead?

Another object flew toward him. He ducked, losing balance. In the time he gained his footing, Rick was over top of him.

The sound of officers rushing toward them was a welcome relief.

A jab to Luke's ribs took his breath away. The blunt end of a shoe cracked into his stomach.

Luke hauled himself into a squatting position, then burst toward Rick, knocking him back a step.

A kick to Rick's groin had him doubled over and groaning.

The fight inside him was still strong, powered by his freeze, fight or flight response. Rick stepped forward, leading with the knife, jabbing at Luke's ribs. He sidestepped and spun in time to avoid direct impact, even though he felt the blade sear through his flesh. There was enough of a wound for blood to ooze through his shirt.

"Not this time, bastard." Luke ignored the pain in order to keep his full focus on Rick.

Another jab caught Luke under the arm.

More of his blood spilled onto the sidewalk.

This time, Luke would be ready when Rick made his move.

"Oh my God, Luke." Julie must've regained consciousness. At least she would be fine.

Luke didn't dare take his gaze off Rick. Another jab and he might just hit something the doctors couldn't fix.

The telltale step forward came, but before Rick could blink, Luke had spun around and twisted the knife. Rick was knocked off balance. He turned in the direction he fell, landing directly on the blade. The knife stabbed him directly through the chest, piercing his heart as footsteps surrounded them.

Rick made a gurgling sound as blood spilled from the side of his mouth and his eyes fixed.

Luke rushed to Julie's side and pulled her into his arms with the intention of never letting go.

Julie's tear-soaked eyes gazed up at him.

He pulled back and looked her straight in the eyes. "Everything's fine now. He can't hurt you anymore. You don't have to cry."

She buried her hands in his shirt, pulled back and gasped. "No, Luke. It's not okay. You're hurt."

He felt light-headed, cold and a little nauseated.

A stoic-faced medic parted the crowd, his gaze fixed on Luke.

He took note of Julie's pallor. Blood was everywhere. Blood on her hands, her shirt, in her hair.

*His* blood.

He was fully awake but couldn't make his mouth form words. How did he tell her he was okay? They'd survived. That he was determined to take her home with him where he could take care of her now that this whole ordeal could be put behind them?

He made another move to speak, but darkness was closing in.

The faint sounds of her sweet voice telling him not to die registered.

EMTs blocked his view of her.

Darkness was pulling, tugging.

Fighting against the tide sucking him under and tossing him out to sea took all the energy he could muster.

Luke closed his eyes.

# Chapter Twenty

Luke blinked his eyes open. His head felt as if he'd tied one on last night, except that couldn't be true.

He searched the room for Julie. Found her as she slept in the chair next to his bed. His heart squeezed.

A short dark-haired nurse rushed in. "Someone's finally awake."

"Yeah, guess I needed a good night's sleep."

"Or three."

"You're telling me I've been out for three days?" he asked quietly, trying not to wake Julie.

"Uh-huh." The nurse went to work pushing buttons on beeping machines.

The noise must've stirred Julie, because she rubbed her eyes and yawned.

"Hello, beautiful."

She sat bolt upright. "Luke. Oh, thank goodness you're awake. Are you okay?" Riding a bolt of lightning couldn't have brought her to his side quicker. "How do you feel?"

"Better. My head hurts. Nothing a little aspirin won't heal." And yet, seeing Julie there, waiting, energized his tired body. God help him, but she was the light.

"How do you feel?" the nurse asked.

He wanted to ask if she was the one who'd dragged cotton balls through his mouth, but thought better of it.

Her permanent frown gave him a hint that she wasn't the teasing type.

"You can give me a shot, clean me or bandage me, but I'm taking this lady beside me home." Little did they know, he wouldn't stop there. He'd do whatever it took to defend her and make her his.

He made a move to get out of bed but was instantly met with two sets of hands pushing him down.

"That's not a good idea, Luke." Julie's voice left no room for doubt.

"You should listen to her," the nurse agreed. "Before I make sure you can't."

He put his hands up in the universal sign of surrender. "No harm done."

Recent events flooded him. His thoughts snapped to his friend. "What happened to Garcia?"

"He's good. He was treated overnight and released. Told me to call him as soon as you woke up." Julie leaned toward him. "If you listen to the doctor and do everything he says, I promise to climb under the sheets and keep you warm later."

The nurse grumbled about his blood pressure as Julie located her phone and sent a text.

"Sweetheart, I don't plan to be here later." He looked into her eyes and saw home.

"Where do you plan to go?"

"With you. Home." He hesitated, praying to see a flicker of excitement in her gaze.

Instead, she lowered her lashes, screening her amber hues. "Your brothers have been calling every hour. They might have something to say about where you end up. Gran's worried sick. And coming home with me? I don't know if that's such a good idea, Luke. We've been down that road before. Remember? I thought I could fix everything by sticking in there, but what did I really do? Hoped everything would magically turn out okay. I was scared to death to try to make you talk. I didn't know how. I'm just as much to blame for what happened."

"No."

"Don't say it, Luke." Her forehead creased and he could tell she was concentrating hard on her next words. "I didn't give up. That part's true. But I let you mope around and eventually drown in your own sadness. I should've stomped on the floor until you picked yourself up. What did I do? I let you fall apart right in front of my eyes."

He made a move to speak but was met with her palm.

"It's true. I didn't know what to do, so I hoped and waited. When that didn't work, I let you push me into the divorce."

"I didn't give you much choice."

"People always have choices, Luke. I didn't fight for us before. Not like I should've."

"I appreciate what you're saying—"

"Then don't take all the blame. What happened to us was both our faults. We were young. We both made mistakes. I shouldn't have let you get away with closing yourself off to me."

Her words lifted the burden he'd been carrying on his shoulders for the years they'd been apart. "Have I told you how sexy you are when you're making sense?"

He brought his hand up to her chin. "I understand if you think it's too risky or too fast. But if you give me a second chance to do what I should've done when I first got back, you won't regret it."

"And what should you have done before?"

"Take you in my arms and never let go. No matter how dark my life becomes, you're the light. Instead of turning away from it, ashamed, I should've run toward it, both arms open.

"I was young and stupid…ashamed of myself for being weak. But I've learned a man isn't weak because he cares about the people he loves. Especially when they're taken from him too soon. A real man hangs on to the people he loves with everything inside him, until light fills him again and the darkness is gone."

Tears rolled down her cheeks. His gaze moved to the bandage on her neck and he thought about how easily he could've lost her.

He thumbed them away. "No more tears. I don't want to make you cry again."

"That's beautiful. You're beautiful."

He cracked a smile. "No. I'm not. But you are."

"Luke Campbell, you're the most beautiful man I've ever known. That's the person I fell in love with before. Who I am shamelessly and deeply in love with now."

"I love you, too." Relief washed over him. He had every intention of asking her to marry him when the time was right. And when she agreed to be his bride this time, it would be forever. "Will you move in with me when I get out of here?"

"Yes."

"Just so you understand what I'm asking, I don't do temporary."

"Neither do I."

"As long as we're being clear. I have every intention of making this permanent as soon as you're ready."

"I'll do my best not to make you wait too long."

"Take as long as you need, sweetheart. Like I said, I'm staying put for as long as you let me. I love you. I never stopped. You're the only one for me."

"Good. Because I can't imagine getting sick of you anytime soon." She leaned close enough for their foreheads to touch. "I never plan to stop fighting for us, Luke. I love you too much."

"Do you have any idea how badly I want to kiss you right now?"

She pulled back and said, "Then what's stopping you, Campbell?"

"Toothpaste. I haven't brushed my teeth yet and I don't want to send you out of the room screaming from my breath."

The nurse, who had finished fiddling with the machines, turned toward the door. "You two behave in here. He needs rest."

Julie helped Luke brush his teeth. He took a swallow of water as she placed the supplies on the counter. He opened the covers. "Get over here, Mrs. Campbell."

"Is that a request?"

"Command. Why? Did it work?"

"Very effective tactic, Campbell."

She slipped under the covers with him and he pulled her body flush with his. "I'm afraid we can't do anything with the nurse keeping her eye on us."

He pressed her fingers to his lips and kissed each tip before finding her lips. "We can get to the rest later. And believe me, we will. For now, having you right here, holding you, is all I need."

\* \* \* \* \*

*Look for the final book in Barb Han's*
**THE CAMPBELLS OF CREEK BEND,**
*on sale in February 2015.*
*You'll find it wherever*
*Harlequin Intrigue books are sold!*

# COMING NEXT MONTH FROM

**H** HARLEQUIN

# I N T R I G U E

## Available January 20, 2015

### #1545 CONFESSIONS
*The Battling McGuire Boys* • by Cynthia Eden
Framed for murder, Scarlett Stone is desperate and turns to private investigator—and her former lover—Grant McGuire for help. If Grant is going to keep Scarlett at his side and in his bed, he has to stop the killer on her trail...

### #1546 HEART OF A HERO
*The Specialists: Heroes Next Door*
by Debra Webb & Regan Black
Specialist Will Chase and trail guide Charly Binali race through the Rockies to stop a national security threat. When a single misstep could be their last, Charly must trust her life and her heart to this handsome stranger.

### #1547 DISARMING DETECTIVE
*The Lawmen* • by Elizabeth Heiter
FBI profiler Ella Cortez's hunt for a rapist takes her to the Florida marshes, into the arms of homicide detective Logan Greer, and into the path of a cunning killer. Falling in love could be deadly...or the only way to survive...

### #1548 THE CATTLEMAN
*West Texas Watchmen* • by Angi Morgan
Cattleman Nick Burke and DEA agent Beth Conrad are opposites—but they have to fake an engagement to trap gunrunners on Nick's ranch. Will they overcome their differences to close the case and find a love that is all too real?

### #1549 HARD TARGET
*The Campbells of Creek Bend* • by Barb Han
Border Patrol agent Reed Campbell finds Emily Baker hiding out in a crate of guns smuggled into Texas. He knows keeping her safe will be hard—but keeping his hands to himself might be nearly impossible...

### #1550 COUNTERMEASURES
*Omega Sector* • by Janie Crouch
Omega agent Sawyer Branson was sent to safeguard Dr. Megan Fuller while she neutralized a dangerous weapon that had fallen into enemy hands. Can Sawyer protect her long enough to finish the countermeasure, or will he have to choose between his agency and his heart?

---

**YOU CAN FIND MORE INFORMATION ON UPCOMING HARLEQUIN® TITLES, FREE EXCERPTS AND MORE AT WWW.HARLEQUIN.COM.**

HICNM0115

# REQUEST YOUR FREE BOOKS!
## 2 FREE NOVELS PLUS 2 FREE GIFTS!

# ⊕ HARLEQUIN®
# INTRIGUE®

## BREATHTAKING ROMANTIC SUSPENSE

**YES!** Please send me 2 FREE Harlequin Intrigue® novels and my 2 FREE gifts (gifts are worth about $10). After receiving them, if I don't wish to receive any more books, I can return the shipping statement marked "cancel." If I don't cancel, I will receive 6 brand-new novels every month and be billed just $4.74 per book in the U.S. or $5.24 per book in Canada. That's a savings of at least 14% off the cover price! It's quite a bargain! Shipping and handling is just 50¢ per book in the U.S. and 75¢ per book in Canada.* I understand that accepting the 2 free books and gifts places me under no obligation to buy anything. I can always return a shipment and cancel at any time. Even if I never buy another book, the two free books and gifts are mine to keep forever.                   182/382 HDN F42N

Name _____ (PLEASE PRINT) _____

Address _____ Apt. # _____

City _____ State/Prov. _____ Zip/Postal Code _____

Signature (if under 18, a parent or guardian must sign)

Mail to the **Harlequin® Reader Service:**
**IN U.S.A.:** P.O. Box 1867, Buffalo, NY 14240-1867
**IN CANADA:** P.O. Box 609, Fort Erie, Ontario  L2A 5X3
**Are you a subscriber to Harlequin Intrigue books
and want to receive the larger-print edition?
Call 1-800-873-8635 or visit www.ReaderService.com.**

* Terms and prices subject to change without notice. Prices do not include applicable taxes. Sales tax applicable in N.Y. Canadian residents will be charged applicable taxes. Offer not valid in Quebec. This offer is limited to one order per household. Not valid for current subscribers to Harlequin Intrigue books. All orders subject to credit approval. Credit or debit balances in a customer's account(s) may be offset by any other outstanding balance owed by or to the customer. Please allow 4 to 6 weeks for delivery. Offer available while quantities last.

**Your Privacy**—The Harlequin® Reader Service is committed to protecting your privacy. Our Privacy Policy is available online at www.ReaderService.com or upon request from the Harlequin Reader Service.

We make a portion of our mailing list available to reputable third parties that offer products we believe may interest you. If you prefer that we not exchange your name with third parties, or if you wish to clarify or modify your communication preferences, please visit us at www.ReaderService.com/consumerschoice or write to us at Harlequin Reader Service Preference Service, P.O. Box 9062, Buffalo, NY 14269. Include your complete name and address.

HI13R

"I need you," she told him as she wet her lips. "I'm desperate, and without your help…I don't know what's going to happen." She glanced over her shoulder, her nervous stare darting to the door.

"Scarlett?" Her fear was palpable, and it made his muscles tense.

"They'll be coming for me soon. I only have a few minutes, and please, *please* stick to your promise. No matter what they say."

He shot away from his desk, his relaxed pose forgotten as he realized that Scarlett wasn't just afraid. She was terrified. "Who's coming?"

"I didn't do it." She rose, too, and dropped her bag into her chair. "It will look like I did, all the evidence says so…but I didn't do it."

He stepped toward her, touched her and felt the jolt slide all the way through him. Ten years…*ten years*…and it was still there. The awareness. The need.

Did she feel it, too?

*Focus.* "Slow down," Grant told her, trying to keep his voice level and calm. "Just take it easy. You're safe here." *With me.*

But that wasn't exactly true. She was in the most danger when she was with him. Only Scarlett had never realized that fact.

"Say you'll help me," she pleaded. Her tone was desperate. She had a soft voice, one that was perfect for whispering in the dark. A voice that had tempted a boy…and sure as hell made the man he'd become think sinful thoughts.

"I'll help you," Grant heard himself say instantly. So he still had the same problem—he couldn't deny her anything.

Her shoulders sagged in apparent relief. "You've changed." Then her hand rose. Her fingers skimmed over his jaw, rasping against the five o'clock shadow that roughened his face. They were so close right then. And memories collided between them.

When she'd been eighteen, he'd always been so careful with her. He'd had to maintain his control at every moment. But that control had broken one summer night, weeks after her eighteenth birthday…

*I can still feel her around me.*

"Grant?"

She wasn't eighteen any longer.

And his control—

He heard voices then, coming from the lobby.

"Keep your promise," Scarlett said.

*What the hell?*

He pulled away from her and walked toward the door.

Those voices were louder now. Because they were…shouting for Scarlett?

*"Scarlett Stone…!"*

"They were behind me." Her words rushed out. "I knew they were closing in, but I wanted to get to you."

He hated the fear in her voice. "You're safe."

"No, I'm not."

*Find out what happens next in*
**CONFESSIONS**
*by* New York Times *bestselling author*
*Cynthia Eden, available February 2015 wherever*
*Harlequin Intrigue® books and ebooks are sold.*

# JUST CAN'T GET ENOUGH
# ROMANCE
## Looking for more?

Harlequin has everything from contemporary, passionate and heartwarming to suspenseful and inspirational stories.

Whatever your mood,
we have a romance just for you!

Connect with us to find your next great read,
special offers and more.

Facebook.com/HarlequinBooks
Twitter.com/HarlequinBooks
HarlequinBlog.com
Harlequin.com/Newsletters

HARLEQUIN®

A *Romance* FOR EVERY MOOD™

www.Harlequin.com